BALLAD OF A SLOPSUCKER

BALLAD OF A
SLOPSUCKER

stories

Juan Alvarado Valdivia

UNIVERSITY OF NEW MEXICO PRESS | ALBUQUERQUE

© 2019 by Juan Alvarado Valdivia
All rights reserved. Published 2019
Printed in the United States of America

Library of Congress Cataloging-in-Publication Data

Names: Alvarado Valdivia, Juan, 1979– author.
Title: Ballad of a slopsucker : stories / Juan Alvarado Valdivia.
Description: Albuquerque : University of New Mexico Press, 2019. |
    Identifiers: LCCN 2018030502 (print) | LCCN 2018030638 (e-book) |
    ISBN 9780826360588 (e-book) | ISBN 9780826360571 (pbk. : alk.
    paper)
Classification: LCC PS3601.L86667 (e-book) | LCC PS3601.L86667 A6
    2019 (print) | DDC 813/.6—dc23
LC record available at https://lccn.loc.gov/2018030502

Cover illustration by Rebeca Garcia-Gonzalez
Designed by Felicia Cedillos
Composed in Melior LT Std 9.75/14

for Maria

Freedom is what you do with what's been done to you.

—JEAN-PAUL SARTRE

Contents

JUSTO

I was lying on my stomach on top of a moving blanket in the trunk of the old Cadillac DeVille I had salvaged. The barrel of my rifle—a Bushmaster M4 XM-15—was sticking ever so slightly out of the trunk from an incision I cut over the license plate. My glow-in-the-dark watch read 12:56 a.m., less than ten minutes after the last train had passed. (I had left my cell phone at home. I wasn't going to be foolish like those Boston Marathon bombers who used their phones as they walked around the finish line.) A hooded man approached the bicycle I had planted behind the Ashby station. Two streetlamps illuminated the shadowy parking lot. The lot was empty except for him and me—but he didn't know this.

Beside the Cannondale I left as bait was a carcass of a bicycle; its tires, chain wheel, and seat post had been stripped. Because I had been lying in the pitch-dark trunk for over an hour, my eyes had adjusted to the night. I could see him survey the parking lot and neighboring street for pedestrians. I had parked at the back of the lot, away from any security cameras pointed at the building's perimeter. He stared at my car for a second before he took out a bolt cutter tucked beneath his sweater. He was fast, decisive. A professional thief, not some junkie in Berkeley looking to steal and sell a bike for a quick fix. A shot to his back would implode his vital organs. About as effective as a head shot.

I slipped on the shooting earplugs dangling from my neck. Squinting, I trained the front sight of my rifle on his lower back. My heart pounded. Like my father had taught me when I was a young boy learning to fire a rifle on our campo, I took a deep breath to still me. This was for the last bicycle stolen from me. This was for the malparido hijueputa who mugged my mother at gunpoint. This was for all the pieces of shit who have ruined this beautiful world that the Lord gave us. My left hand held the rifle by its forestock. My finger jittered on the trigger. I exhaled so loud that I was afraid the thief would hear my breath echo in the car trunk, so I pulled the trigger, fired the gun, and felt it recoil against my shoulder. He crumbled next to the bike.

It didn't seem real—that I had shot a person. I had shot a few ducks and an armadillo as a teenager, but never a human. It was the most exhilarating moment of my life. My heart was thumping hard inside my chest, then I felt the weight of the rifle in my hands—all seven pounds of it—and I snapped out of my spell. I slithered out of the trunk to the folded-down back seat. I wanted to fling the trunk open and stalk over to him and yank his head off the ground by his hair and say, "For stealing from another, maldito cerote," before I'd kick his teeth in. But I had to make a getaway. The shot had boomed off the building, pierced through the neighborhood.

He was my first.

There was no one in sight as I parked in the garage. I noticed the creaking sound of the car door as I opened it, the tap of my sneakers on the concrete while I stepped out, the muffled click as I gently closed the door, and the sound of my steps as I walked across the dimly lit garage. Everything felt heightened. Inherently dramatic. On my way to the stairwell I looked over at the gate, half-expecting a police car to roar up to it, its red and blue lights flashing and spinning. But there was no one there. No one around. I bounded the stairs and made it to my apartment without being seen.

Inside, I couldn't wind down. I felt electric. My pulse was racing. I downed two shots of rum and ate some chips on the couch.

I hardly slept that night. I lay in bed until about four in the morning, staring at the faint crack of streetlight that trickled through the curtains. I kept waiting for a SWAT team to pound the door down and storm my apartment, their red infrared lasers pointing into my bedroom. I stayed up so late, feeling half-awake and half-asleep until I found myself on my knees at the foot of the bed, praying, *Please Lord, have mercy on me*, over and over again. I slipped back into bed. A loaded handgun lay on my nightstand. Before long my thoughts began to slow. *You got away with it*, I kept hearing in my head until I realized that *I had* because I'd been lying in my bed for hours. The Lord had answered my prayers. Then I slept a dreamless sleep.

Tuesday morning, the day after the shooting, the *Oakland Tribune* and *San Francisco Chronicle* ran small online articles about the bicycle thief I had gunned down.

He was a Caucasian male in his early twenties. An employee from the Ed Roberts Campus discovered his body around 7:15 in the morning. Both articles said the police "speculated that the victim was attempting to steal a bicycle found at the scene since a bolt cutter was tied to a string around his neck." Later, a CBS-5 evening news report I watched from my apartment stated that my victim was gunned down with "a high-powered assault rifle." The police had no leads but suspected that the victim was gunned down in the process of stealing a bike.

The bicycles I was planting had been purchased at flea markets five months before. Their serial numbers had already been removed. Their frames and parts had been wiped clean of any fingerprints with Windex and a cloth. The police would have nothing to lead them to me. Once a second victim was gunned down in two days' time, those good-for-nothing thieves might think twice about stealing any bicycle at night, fearful it might be a booby trap.

And my experiment, for the time being, would be a success.

Where could I say it all began? With the first bicycle stolen from me seven years ago when I lived in a small apartment in Hayward with my parents and another Nicaraguan family? Or was it the time the wheels from my bike were stolen when I locked it outside the Lake Merritt station? Or did it all begin because of my ex-girlfriend, Brenda, who was the one who got me into cycling in the first place? Where does anything truly begin?

My plans to hunt bicycle thieves first began six months ago after a date with a cute half-Mexican girl. She had invited me over to her place for the first time. She lived at an apartment up on Adams Point, one of the safer neighborhoods in Oakland. Since we met after work, I had my trusty companion with me—a sleek Bianchi street bike. I parked my bike in her apartment's garage, figuring that would be safer than leaving it locked out on the street. I didn't expect to spend the night with her, but I did. The next morning, I returned to the garage to find my bike— which had two U-locks to secure both tires and the frame—was gone. The locks, warped and bent, lay on the ground like a "fuck you" from the thieves. She felt awful. She offered to drop me off at my apartment in East Oakland. I refused. I needed to walk it off.

Once I walked two blocks down the hill, which was lined with apartments, I saw no one around. I screamed. I screamed so loud it felt like my temples could burst. My arms shook from anger. As I stalked toward Grand Avenue, I kept thinking of how I didn't know what buses to take home. I was so used to cycling the three and a half miles from my apartment to the recycling center I worked at in West Oakland. I had no need to know the local bus system. Not with my bicycle.

Once on a bus, I sat near the back, glaring out the window. I kept picturing that filthy thief sneaking into the garage in the early morning, patiently prying open my U-locks with a car jack. That fucking asshole. Who would fuck with someone's bike—especially one that couldn't make them that much money?

And then, not even two days later, my father called to tell me that my mother was in the hospital. She had been mugged on a residential street a few blocks from their apartment in San Leandro. She was walking home with a bag of groceries when a car rolled up next to her. A young black man with a baseball hat and sunglasses rolled down the passenger window and pointed a gun at her. He told her to hand over her purse. My mother complied, then sneered at him and said, "Sinvergüenza." The little fucking hood rat shot her in the leg before they sped off. The shot splintered my mother's femur, and she injured her hip when she fell on the sidewalk. The doctors told us she'll never walk the same again. Not at her age.

Alongside my father I attended church for the first time in years. How could God allow such bad things to happen to decent people? How could He allow bad people to get away with these crimes? I sought answers to these questions.

Weeks passed. I continued to attend services, seeking some answer. In my desperation I sought confession. In the dark booth I asked the priest, "Why does God allow such things?" As I expected, he told me that it was not our place to question the ways of the Lord. Everything happens for a divine reason, he told me. The Lord has His ways of testing us, His way of directing us down our path. Before I trudged out of the church, I lifted my head, turned to the altar, and crossed myself. I was not sure if my questions had any answers.

Later that night while I cycled home on my latest bike—a dinged-up road bicycle hardly worth stealing—a thought came to me, as if from the heavens. It dawned on me that the Lord *can* move in mysterious ways—through each of us, including myself. Each one of us is an extension of God. Then it all came to me: buying used bikes as bait to lure those wretched thieves; obtaining a car to use as a mobile sniper nest like John Allen Muhammad; buying a rifle through a family friend and using it to gun down five people—two for the scoundrels who harmed my mother and three for the number of bicycles that had been stolen from me. The world was full of people who didn't deserve to live—people who wouldn't hesitate to lie and manipulate others to gain or maintain power; people who wouldn't hesitate to exploit others for more wealth; people who wouldn't hesitate to harm and take from another. Bicycle thieves are petty, at the bottom of that chain, but they were a group *I* could do something about.

I would exact the Lord's justice through my own hands. After all, my name *is* Justo.

♦

Early Thursday morning, 1:18 a.m. Corner of 9th and Howard. I spotted my next victim while I lay in the car trunk, parked across the street from the bike I had planted. A young white man with cropped hair walked up to the bike, which was locked to a parking meter. He looked at it, took out his cell phone, and stepped over to a nearby alley. The street was barren. Only homeless vagrants and occasional late-night revelers roamed those streets. From time to time a drone of cars motored down 9th Street toward Market. A few cars drove into the Chevron on the corner. There were no pedestrians passing by.

Seven minutes after he hid in the alley, a hooded man cycling on Howard Street rolled up onto the sidewalk. He dismounted as his friend stepped out of the alley.

Together, like a routine they had performed countless times, the one with the bicycle parked his bike alongside the one I had planted. He turned his back to the street to obscure any passing motorists or cyclists. A white overhead light shone above them. I could see them clearly. His friend started making a sawing motion. By that point, I could hear my heart hammering as I slipped my earplugs on. Like a snake preparing to strike, the rifle barrel peeked out of the trunk. I turned my sights on both of them—first the head of the taller man with cropped hair, then the chest area of his accomplice. I could feel myself fill with something like glee as I turned the rifle's front sight from one to the other then back again like a game of Eenie Meenie Miney Mo. I couldn't decide which one to shoot. Who did the Lord want me to strike down? I longed to shoot them both—two birds with one stone as they say in this country—but I did not have much practice shooting one target then quickly shifting to another. I picked eenie—the hard shot.

Once I fixed the front sight on the back of his head, I pulled the trigger. The right side of his head exploded, bursting like a watermelon I had once blown up with an explosive. His friend jolted from the deafening shot and then held his hands up and shrieked as he saw his friend's body topple over the bicycle. He tore off down the sidewalk. I fired and missed, shattering a window behind him as he ran screaming for help. As he darted toward the corner, he ran into an open space between two parked cars. I trained my sight on that spot and waited for him to run into it. I fired two rounds. He fell, skidding face first to the pavement at the corner. His howling pierced the streets.

Past the intersection I saw a man standing beside his car as he fueled up at the gas station. He craned his head around the car to look in the direction of the screaming. He must have seen the hooded man lying on the sidewalk because he ducked behind his car—to call the police, I presumed.

After I thumbed the safety into its locked position, I slithered back out of the trunk, past the back seat, and hurdled myself between the front seats. Behind the wheel, I turned the ignition and looked at the side mirror to see if anyone was following. To my fortune—the Lord's divine hand at work again—the signal turned green for northbound traffic on 9th Street. A few cars drove along the street as I turned the Cadillac—without my lights on—onto Howard Street. Once beyond eyesight of the 9th and Howard intersection, I gunned the big car down the grimy street, made a screeching right on 11th Street, a left on Mission, and another left onto South Van Ness, all the while looking in the rearview mirror until I made it to the on-ramp.

From the freeway the city's skyline unfolded before me. I eased my foot off the gas. I flicked the radio on and turned the dial to the oldies station. I looked at the rosary beads dangling from the rearview mirror. I crossed myself. "Gracias Diosito," I said. "Gracias."

Before long, I approached the tunnel at Treasure Island. No police lights flashed behind me. "Be Thankful for What You Got" came on the radio. The tunnel's orange light poured over my hands on the steering wheel. I bobbed my head to the music. I slapped the dashboard and laughed. *This is nice*, I thought. *Real nice*. It'd been four years since I'd owned a gas-guzzling vehicle—and I was aware of the irony of utilizing it to slaughter bicycle thieves. The 1982 blue-gray Cadillac DeVille fell into my possession a month after my mother was assaulted. I had rescued it from a junkyard that partnered with my employer. From the moment I laid my eyes on the Cadillac with its large trunk that could easily conceal my five-foot-four frame, I knew what I would use it for. It was a godsend.

I had renounced owning a vehicle after my then-girlfriend, Brenda, told me about the drilling waste Chevron left in Ecuador that polluted the Amazon where a few of her distant family members lived. Her uncle and cousin, who fished in the polluted river, died from a pancreatic cancer—a disease no one from the tribe had before Petroecuador and Texaco began drilling in the 1960s. And, of course, once they got what they wanted, the oil company left with their riches and left a toxic mess for the poor brown people of a "developing nation" to deal with. Typical of white people. It's like they have it in their blood to be exploiters. Leeches. Parasites.

With an arm eased over the steering wheel, I crossed the bridge with oldies playing from the radio. The car and I were perfect conspirators.

The second slaying generated much more media coverage. One killing can be a whim, but a second is devotion. Plus, my second shooting netted two victims. The second man I shot was in critical condition. As for the first guy, the *San Francisco Chronicle* only reported that he had been "shot in the head," not that much of it had been blown off or that the police probably had to wipe chunks of his brain off the sidewalk. Despite occurring in a downtown street next to a gas station, there was—apparently, God willing—no sighting of my car.

The police suspected that both shootings were related. The San Francisco and Berkeley Police Departments had concluded that the bicycles found at the scene had been left as bait for would-be bicycle thieves. Though anticipated, this concerned me. One fingerprint, one single DNA sample *anywhere* on either bicycle could be the end for me. But I had been thorough in wiping off every single part of those bicycles and their locks before handling them with wiped-off gloves. The bike locks I bought were standard OnGuard U-locks that could not be traced to a particular bicycle shop or sporting goods store. I had slid off the plastic parts that had a serial number on them. I had not been dumb enough to purchase any of them with a credit card.

To my surprise and delight, a few of the commenters for the online articles came close to condoning my actions. (I only read online articles from public computers at the library.) One of the most popular comments read, "Can't say I'm sorry for these lowlifes. Not cool to steal someone's bike." Another comment read, "Now if only this vigilante would go after the people who keep breaking into my car!" Another read, "Just keep it to the bicycle thieves." One comment with lots of thumbs-up votes read, "Well at least SOMEONE'S doing something about bicycle theft because SFPD sure ain't." I couldn't help but grin when I read those comments.

Over the weekend I laid low. I was still having trouble sleeping, waking every few hours with anxiety dreams that were absent of police officers closing in on me but were nevertheless full of tension and panicked situations, like one dream in which I had five minutes to go into a grocery store to buy all my food for the week before the store blew up. I'd pick up on my killing spree the following week once I returned to work after my vacation. But, in the meantime, I was too curious to see what effects, if any, my slayings had on the bicycle sellers at the local flea markets.

It was a sunny summer afternoon at the Laney College Flea Market. Like I had on my bicycle-buying missions to other flea markets months before, I wore a baseball cap and dark sunglasses. After I bought some pupusas, I zigzagged through the crowd on my way to the largest bicycle seller. At these markets it was common knowledge that most if not all the used bikes for sale had been stolen. Only foolish thieves attempted to sell bikes hot off the streets. Most professional thieves—from what I read—amassed a collection of stolen bicycles to sell on a run to LA through the internet.

The three men selling the largest selection of bikes at the flea market had the usual amount for sale—about eight to ten bikes. Two of the men lounged on lawn chairs resting on their raised platform. They were tough-looking guys—blue-collar types who probably got dumb on a steady diet of beer and baseball. I looked over some of the bikes, garnering the attention of one of the larger men.

"These prices set?" I asked.

"Some are negotiable," he said.

I stepped over to a Bianchi mountain bike. A price tag dangling from the steering handle read $125. Its blue color reminded me of my old stolen bike.

"That's a nice bike," I said.

The man took a step forward. "Price on that one isn't negotiable. Those tires and rims are practically new."

I bent over to look at the brake pads. Shimano parts. Slightly worn. I would have been enraged if this bike were stolen from me.

"You heard about the guy who's gunning down bicycle thieves?" I asked.

"Nope."

"Really? It's been all over the news. You from here?"

"You interested in that bike or not, buddy?"

I stood up, took a step toward him. "You can't tell me where these fine bicycles came from, can you?" I said.

His burly friend with a beer gut looked over at us. "You want the bike or not?" he said, crossing his arms, looking down at me.

I grinned, pushed my sunglasses down enough to see him eye to eye. "You're not worried that this vigilante might be checking you all out?" I asked. "Watching you sell your legitimately attained goods? Because if I were you, *I'd* be worried."

Smiling, I raised my brows a few times at him and turned to leave. He stepped off the platform. He shoved me in the back. "What the fuck's your problem, buddy?" he said.

I walked off, holding my hands out for the group of onlookers staring at us. Then I pointed my fingers like guns at them—boom boom boom—and left.

Days later I was at it again. I parked the Cadillac in a parking lot next to the post office in downtown Oakland. The only buildings on that block were two businesses with no windows looking out onto Alice Street and the stately post office. I figured there was little chance anyone would catch my spider-catching-a-fly act. The only nearby building with residents was the Hotel Oakland, which was used for senior housing.

For this one I decided to change things up. One, I planned to recover the planted bicycle; no more leaving evidence for the cops. Two, in its place I would leave a self-made tarot card of Death riding a horse next to the body of my victim. Three, since these surrounding downtown streets were mostly vacant early at night, I would attempt to conduct my killing before midnight. Any variable—from an initial shooting in Berkeley then San Francisco then Oakland—would help to baffle the pigs. I would have to be out of there soon, though. With a pattern of killings established, I had to assume that all the local police departments—even one as inept and undermanned as the Oakland Police Department—would establish immediate blockades within a half-mile radius of the shooting once it was reported. The Montgomery County police utilized this tactic to try to catch the Beltway Sniper.

For bait I tied a shiny, brand-new-looking Diamondhead mountain bike to a street sign with a thin cable. I was betting that this would be enough to lure a thief searching for an easy bike to steal.

At about 11:25 p.m., after waiting in the trunk since

9:40 p.m., two dark men walked by. They were drunk—laughing and conversing in an African language. Half an hour later an old white man, muttering to himself, looked at the bike as he pushed his shopping cart full of junk down the street. He didn't stop to try to steal the bike. I'm not sure if I would've shot him. I wasn't out to get people who were already discarded by this inhumane capitalist system. That's not what the Lord would want from me.

I nodded off for a while, holding the rifle against my chest. It was not unlike the night watches I used to have with my father on our ranch in León when the Contras—who were funded by the American government—marched around our country, setting fire to the homes and fields of citizens they suspected of being Sandinista loyalists. And then, around 12:30 a.m., an old Datsun rolled up next to the bicycle. The driver killed the lights. I was jolted awake. Two men sat in the front. The one in the passenger seat, beside the bike, studied the cable lock. They looked around for a good while. Did they sense that it appeared too easy? If he hesitated to steal the bike, I stumbled as well when he opened the car door, triggering its interior light. He was a young, baby-faced Latino. He reminded me of one of my cousins back in Nicaragua.

He walked to the back of the car, out of view. I heard the trunk open. He stepped back into my line of fire, holding a small bolt cutter. I was parked twenty-five feet away. A can't-miss shot.

He snapped the cable with little effort. He bent over to twist off the front wheel. I had the front sight locked on his back, but I couldn't push myself to pull the trigger. Seeing him reminded me of when my family and I first came to this country in asylum, fleeing the civil war. Near

15

the end of our first year in the United States I began to rummage through supermarket dumpsters at night with a friend to feed our families. Perhaps these thieves were like us when we first came to this country.

I made a glancing shot of his calf. He fell to the ground next to a tree, screaming and clutching his leg. His partner crouched out of sight and revved the motor. The young man I shot dragged himself back toward the passenger door. "¡No me dejes, Armando!" he yelled, frantically waving his hand. "¡No me dejes!" The car lurched forward so the man could grab the door handle. I had my front sights on his chest, the area above his heart. He opened the door and raised himself up onto the seat with his arms and good leg—and I just watched him. Ducking in their seats, they sped off before he even shut the door. I waited a few seconds before I scurried over to retrieve the bicycle. I saw no one walking on Alice Street or in front of the post office. A few windows were alit in the Oakland Hotel across the street from the parking lot, but they were up on the top floors. I chucked the bike into the trunk and motored onto Jackson Street to the freeway.

Speeding down 880, I pounded the steering wheel and screamed. Two bicycle thieves had walked away with their lives. The Lord gave me a test, and I had allowed my emotions to get the better of me. It was the kind of mistake that got assassins caught.

The morning news reported that an unidentified man told the police he witnessed what might have been a shooting from the "Bicycle Thief Sniper," as the media had dubbed me. He had been walking along the back of the post office when he slipped behind some bushes, presumably to urinate. He heard a loud shot across the street, heard the young Latino screaming for help. Fearing for his life, the witness remained hidden behind the tall bushes next to the post office. He saw me grab and toss the bicycle into the trunk. He described me as a short, stocky man in a dark-gray hoodie. He couldn't tell what ethnicity I was, but he did see my blue-gray Cadillac haul out of the parking lot. The police put an alert out for my car.

That night, under the cover of dark, I drove the car to my friend Victor. He owned an auto body shop in Hayward. Money up front, no questions asked, I told him to paint the car a tan color. I could trust him. Victor was a family friend—and he was un narcotraficante. When I asked him for a black-market assault rifle, his cousin was the one who sold me the XM-15.

Victor took the car in for a few days, which eased my worries about having it noticed in my apartment garage. But when I came to pick it up, one of his cronies—a short, barrel-chested man with a dark complexion and a long goatee—walked over to me. He was wiping his hands with an oily rag.

"You know, that car looks a lot like the one the police keep mentioning in that sniper case," he said with a heavy Spanish accent.

I turned to Victor.

"Are you the guy?" he said, staring at me, turning his head with a mischievous grin.

"What are you talking about?" I said.

He put his hands on his hips and laughed. "You are the guy! Wow. The boogeyman, en vivo!"

"¿Que te pasa, mamaberga?" I said, balling up my fists as Victor stepped between us.

17

"It's all right, Justo. This is Carlitos. He likes to fuck with people."

"Yeah, no te preocupes," Carlitos said. "Your secret's safe with me . . . for the right price."

"What does he mean for the right price?" I said to Victor.

Carlitos glared at me. "It means you pay up, cochon," he sneered.

"Does he do this with every customer?" I said to Victor. My head began to feel hot, like my temples were being pressed together.

"You can talk to me, hijueputa," Carlitos said, taking a step toward me.

"Just give him a tip," Victor said. "He's the one who worked on your car."

I glared back at Carlitos. "All I have on me is about seventeen dollars."

"Well you better get some more," Victor said in a flat voice while Carlitos puckered his lips and nodded.

Once I cycled out of the garage I took a deep breath. The muscles between my shoulders felt tight. I wiped sweat from my forehead. Victor's men were people you didn't want to fuck with.

I rolled back to Victor's garage with two hundred dollars in hand. Carlitos was hunched over the motor of a car. Once he heard me he peered around the propped-up hood. He wiped his brow as I marched up to him. I held out a hundred-dollar bill between two fingers. He snatched it and had the audacity to hold it up to see if it was real.

"Victor might need you for a favor, so keep up your target practice," he said.

On the ride home I felt an enormous relief simply driving the car. I wasn't checking the rearview mirror every couple of seconds like I had when I first drove to Victor's garage, fearful a police car would recognize the Cadillac and signal to pull over. With its dull-tan color, it no longer resembled the car they were looking for. That pinche Carlitos might still hit me up for a bribe, but the Lord had spared me again. That's how I knew He still had work for me to carry out.

A week later I struck again. Killed two punk Latinos—probably fucking Mexicans—trying to steal my planted bike over by Park Boulevard near 580. I considered it a makeup for the previous shooting I botched. I had no mercy on those hoodlums, rained a few automatic rounds to get them. The pavement was caked in blood.

By then, with four separate shootings, the online commenters were no longer supportive of my actions. They got hung up on how young the last victims were: sixteen and eighteen years of age. That made no difference to me. They were old enough to know that stealing was a sin. Why else did they wear dark clothes and hoodies at night? They're the same pissed-off, uneducated cowards who are going around mugging upstanding citizens like my mother at gunpoint. Their parents should have done a better job raising those porquerías de mierda, but that's not my fucking problem. I was just helping to clean up the mess they seeded.

With that latest slaying, I reached my original goal of five victims.

So I stopped.

Or at least I tried.

The weeks passed without incident. The police never came sniffing after me, although all the news headlines were about the manhunt. I hid the rifle in an area that could not be traced back to me. I rid my apartment of any articles related to the slayings. I pulled a trunk lid from another Cadillac DeVille at a Pick-n-Pull and used it to replace the one I had gutted for my car's sniper nest. After I scrapped the incriminating car piece and cleaned out the trunk, I sold the car to a laborer from Stockton. I had cleansed myself of those crimes.

And then, one day, a coworker told me our receptionist, Sunny—a fine Vietnamese woman who had immigrated to the United States two years before—had been fired. All of us men, no matter our race, loved that woman. She was kind, always cheerful in person or over the phone. We used to joke about who would take her home to be their wife. The rumor was that the big boss, a fat old man named Jim, fired her because she rejected his advances.

A few days after I heard this, I walked through our small office. Jim had already hired a new receptionist. Another young Asian woman. I introduced myself to her before I walked into the break room. Jim was pouring himself a cup of coffee from the thermos. He was dressed like a typical bigwig: button-down shirt, blue slacks, polished shoes, a striped tie. Though he heard me walk in, he didn't bother to turn around to say hello. Just continued fixing his coffee—opening a creamer packet then pouring some sugar, all while blocking me from reaching the thermos. Typical gringo—taking up space like they own the world.

I could feel myself get hot inside as I waited for him to step aside. When I stared up at the back of his pale neck, gleaming beneath the fluorescent light, I imagined how easy it would be to walk up behind him and slit that privileged, double-chinned throat of his with my hunting knife. That silk tie of his would be ruined.

Two weeks later I am walking through the office after everyone has left. I step over to the receptionist's desk. I sift through a drawer, searching for the key she uses to lock up the personnel files. To my fortune it is not difficult to find. She keeps it tucked in the back of a hanging folder near the front of the drawer. The Lord left it easy to find. That's how I know it's part of His plan for me.

Like I saw her do a week before when I asked to look at my W-4 form, I take the key to open the file cabinet outside Jim's office. And there I find it—his personnel file. Within a matter of seconds, I find his address.

He will never suspect a thing.

A PEDESTRIAN QUESTION

"**W**ell, there goes LACMA," Gabriel wanted to say to his friend Eric as they motored down Wilshire Boulevard while a ferocious Mastodon song blared from the speakers. Eric didn't even slow the car to glance at the tourists and hipsters posing by the peculiar rows of streetlamps in front of the museum. When they planned their summer road trip—their first one without their parents—Gabriel suggested a trip to LACMA or the Getty. The Getty had a landscaped garden, panoramic vistas of Los Angeles, and it was free. But Eric crinkled his mouth at Gabriel's suggestion. "Nah, dude," Eric said, "that sounds like some gay shit." Instead they were heading to Hollywood to check out the Walk of Fame. Viewing art masterpieces was "gay," but staring at stars on slabs of concrete apparently was not. Gabriel couldn't protest, though. He also couldn't flick through SoCal's radio stations to discover some new music—something other than Mastodon, Static-X, and all the aggressive music

Eric had blasted during their trip. It was Eric's car. His music to listen to. And Gabriel was along for the ride.

Before long, Eric drove his dingy Hyundai into a parking lot near Hollywood Boulevard. As he stepped out of the car, Gabriel stared up at a tall building; they didn't have those in Fremont—the forgettable Northern California suburb they called home. Gabriel clopped along beside Eric in his flip-flops. With his long eyelashes and boyish good looks, Gabriel looked like the token Latino model for a summer-wear catalog in his dark-blue khaki shorts and button-down shirt.

A pair of young women sauntered in their direction. Eric straightened his baggy Oakland A's jersey. He stared at the petite blonde through his dark sunglasses. Coupled with his short, spiky hair, Gabriel thought those glasses made his friend look like a bro-doucher in the making.

"I'd split her in half," Eric said, once the girls walked past them.

"Her friend was cute," Gabriel said, as though he were explaining that cars ran on fuel.

They turned onto Hollywood Boulevard, stepping past a parade of slow-footed window-shoppers and sidewalk gawkers. As they approached a liquor store, Gabriel noticed two guys step outside. He tried not to stare at the statuesque one with crystal-blue eyes, broad shoulders, and tanned arms. Sometimes he couldn't help it, even around his best friend.

After they toured the Walk of Fame and Dolby Theater, Gabriel and Eric puttered around Hollywood. Gabriel bought a *Star Wars* poster at a tourist shop. Eric purchased souvenir shot glasses even though they couldn't legally drink. At a smoke shop with a cardboard cutout of George Burns holding a box of cigars, Gabriel chuckled as they took turns posing with it, but then Eric stood next to it, pumping his fist to his mouth and pushing his cheek out with his tongue while making a slurping sound. Inside, Gabriel cringed, but he managed to laugh off his friend's antics.

Side by side they ambled down Sunset Boulevard on their way to an In-N-Out Burger. Half a block ahead they spotted a cameraman and a woman standing on the sidewalk outside a strip mall.

"Ooh, they're filming something," Gabriel said.

"What do you think they're filming?"

Gabriel and Eric picked up their pace. They could see that the young woman standing in front of the camera was holding a long microphone.

"Dude, I think they're interviewing people," Eric said.

"Thank god I showered today," Gabriel said, combing the side of his head with his fingers.

As they approached, the young woman turned to them. She wore a blue summer dress and bookish glasses.

"Hey guys, how's it going?" she asked.

"We're good," Eric said. "What are you filming?"

"Jimmy Kimmel Live. Pedestrian Question segment. You two interested?"

"Hell yeah!"

"Okay, cool," she said, pointing the shotgun microphone at Eric as the videographer pivoted the camera toward him. "So, what are your names and where are you from?"

Eric leaned into the microphone.

"I'm Eric, and I'm from Fremont, California."

"And I am Gabriel, and I'm also from Fremont."

"And are you a gay couple or straight friends?" she asked.

Gabriel looked at Eric.

"We're straight," Eric said, crossing his arms.

"Okay, thanks guys. Now, we just need you to sign some video release forms. This doesn't guarantee that you will be on the show, but we do need your consent to be considered."

She handed them clipboards and pens. Eric signed the bottom of the form without reading it. Gabriel hesitated. He read the disclaimer. Once Eric handed the clipboard back to her, Gabriel scribbled his signature.

Gabriel and Eric walked halfway down the block in silence. Gabriel noticed that Eric walked a step further from him than he had all day, or the day before when they strolled along the Santa Monica Promenade.

"Why do you think she asked *us*?" Eric said, a jagged edge in his voice. "Do you think we look gay to her?"

Gabriel furrowed his brow. Eric looked like he was ready to tailgate in his long denim shorts, high-top sneakers, and baseball jersey.

"She's just asking everyone . . . or at least groups of the same gender who walk past them," Gabriel said. "I think I saw that bit one time on Jimmy Kimmel Live. It's like Jaywalking . . . asking people on the streets questions so their audience can guess their answer. I've seen them ask people if they'd ever had sex on an airplane."

"Okay," Eric said, marching down the street.

Gabriel was quiet as they approached the In-N-Out Burger. He had known Eric since elementary school. They had played on the same little league baseball team. They became best friends during their junior year of high school when they had three classes together. They fell into being best friends. Neither of them fit in with any of the cliques at school. They shared a mutual dislike of grade-grubbers, jocks, and the vapid pretty girls who relied on their good looks for their popularity. Together they honed the art of sarcasm, as well as burping on cue.

After placing their orders Gabriel and Eric sat on a bench to wait for their burgers. Gabriel watched Eric as he scoped out the line for attractive women. Once he spotted one—a Latina with taut, muscular legs—he nudged Gabriel in the side. Eric nodded in her direction. Gabriel glanced at her and then continued to stare at the workers by the pick-up area. Eric thumped Gabriel in the shoulder.

"What was that for?" Gabriel said.

"You barely looked at that chick I pointed out."

"So what? What's the fucking point? We don't live here so we're never going to see these people again."

"You can still look at them."

Gabriel rolled his eyes. "And what does that accomplish? There are good-looking girls *everywhere*. It's not a big deal. Maybe it is for *you*, but not for me."

They took their trays outside. Despite the umbrella above their table, the sunlight glared off the concrete around them. Eric slipped his sunglasses on as they ate.

"Where should we go after this?" Gabriel asked. He was trying to get past their uncomfortable exchange.

"Don't know," Eric said, taking a bite from his burger. Gabriel stared off at traffic on Sunset Boulevard. "We could roll around downtown or check out Venice Beach."

"Either one sounds good. It's hot as hell. Maybe we should hit the beach?"

"Cool."

Eric wiped his fingers on a napkin. He took a long sip from his drink. He watched Gabriel suck his milkshake from the straw.

"Dude—" Eric said. "Are you gay? You can tell me."

Gabriel could feel his stomach knot.

"I'm *straight*, Eric. Straight as an arrow."

Eric stared back at Gabriel. He felt uncomfortable sitting there—as if a hot, blinding spotlight shined down upon him. It reminded him of the time his mother told him that his father had asked her if he was gay since he never went out with girls. Gabriel snatched his cup of water. He slurped from the straw but stopped when he became self-conscious of how that appeared.

"You sure, man?"

"I'm *sure*."

"Then how come you never talk about girls?"

"Never? You think I *never* talk about girls? Do you even remember our junior year when I took Betsy to the prom, when we made out at the park afterward? Is that not conclusive evidence for you, or are we gonna have to double back to the parking lot and hope we run into those two girls we saw earlier and see if they're interested in fucking us so you can see me stick it to one of them?"

"Okay, okay, dude, I get it," Eric said, rearing back, lifting his hands. "I'm sorry. Sorry I doubted you."

Gabriel recalled their junior prom. He remembered sitting on a bench at Marshall Park while he and Eric passed around a bottle of spiced rum. He could feel Betsy's eyes on him. He knew she wanted to kiss him when she took a slug from the bottle and smiled at him. Gabriel had never kissed a girl. He drank and drank to muster the courage.

He never figured out why he felt so nervous—because it was his first kiss? Because he felt pressured to do it in front of others? Or because he never felt like kissing her?

Gabriel shook his head. "Why are you bringing this up *now*?" he asked.

"I don't know. Because that girl asked us if we were a couple?"

Looking away from Eric, Gabriel drank from his cup of water. They continued to eat without saying a word. Eric had never brought up Gabriel's sexuality before—at least not so directly. For Gabriel it felt like an eternal minute passed before Eric nonchalantly changed the subject and said, "We should hit up a record store before we leave town." Gabriel nearly spewed his mouthful of food to laugh. But instead, he simply thought, *Really? Really?* The dangerous, uncomfortable subject was not brought up again—as though the question had never been uttered.

Later that afternoon Gabriel and Eric strolled down the Venice Beach Boardwalk. The sky was a cloudless blue. The beachside boardwalk was lined with palm trees. A stream of people walked up and down the sidewalk. Eric laughed when they passed a husky man with a long beard who sang John Lennon's "Imagine" off-key while playing on a rainbow-colored acoustic guitar.

"This place is crawling with freaks!" Eric said.

As they walked past a mural portraying Van Gogh's "Starry Night," Gabriel saw two young men holding hands. One was a thin Asian and the other was a fellow Latino. They both wore sunglasses, worn T-shirts, shorts, and flip-flops. What was remarkable about them was how unre-markable they seemed. Back in Fremont, Gabriel never saw gay couples holding hands. It never even struck him as a possibility. But there he was, wandering down the boardwalk in Venice while two young men a few years older than him casually strolled hand in hand for all the world to see—and they looked happy, smiling at all the sights they took in together. Gabriel had not known that gay men could appear so *normal*.

That evening, back in their hotel room, Eric peed in the bathroom with the door locked. With his back against the headboard, Gabriel browsed through photos he had posted on Instagram of their jaunts through Hollywood and Venice Beach. He grinned as he played the video he took of a skater at the skate park by the beach. He would have taken more photos and videos of him, but he was afraid Eric would have thought that was strange, even though he just thought the guy was really good—though he also happened to be handsome in a rebel-skater way.

Yawning, Eric tottered out of the bathroom. He was dressed in the ratty clothes he wore to bed.

"Dude, I'm hella tired," Eric said, flopping face first on his bed.

Eric rolled over to grab the remote control. He turned the TV on. Pointing the control at the screen, he watched a few seconds of each local newscast before clicking through the channels. "There's jack shit on," he said.

Gabriel set his phone on the dresser. His hand was shaking. He sat up straight and stared at the TV as Eric scrolled through the channel guide. His shoulders felt tight. He took a deep breath. He looked over at his friend.

"Have you ever known anyone who's gay?" Gabriel asked.

"I don't think so. Why?"

Gabriel thought of the couple they saw at the board-walk.

"Because I think I am."

Eric stopped clicking through the channels.

"Well I hope you don't think *I* am," Eric said, his eyes glued to the TV.

Gabriel didn't know what to say. Eric turned to him with a hard face.

"Dude, that's some weird shit. Why did you tell me on our last night here?"

"You're my friend, Eric. *My friend.* If I *am* gay, do you think I'm going to sneak into your bed at night when you're asleep? Do you think that's what I want to do? Do you think just because you're a guy that I'm . . . interested in you?"

"So why are you telling me *now*?"

"Because you asked me before and told me I could tell you!"

Gabriel could feel his heart thumping. Eric exhaled loudly.

"Okay, okay. It's just weird, all right."

"What's weird?"

"That you're gay! You're my friend."

"I still am—"

Eric didn't look back at Gabriel. Instead, he stared at a corner of the room. After a while, he took the remote control. With his lips pursed into a tight line, Eric continued to flip through the channels.

Gabriel turned away.

EL CENOTE

El Castillo, the magnificent pyramid in the center of Chichén Itzá, loomed before Javier as he stood on the field surrounding it. He wore a backpack over his damp shirt with a camera bag wrapped around his waist. A throng of tourists clad in bikinis, tank tops, and baggy shorts stood around him. They wore designer sunglasses over their bright-red faces, their arms and chests burnt from the sun. Most of them wore sandals that carried flecks of sand from the beaches they had traveled from. He was dressed similarly—shoes instead of flip-flops— but he was the only one by himself. They grinned as they wandered around, filling the air with chortles and a succession of beeps and clicks from their digital cameras. Javier felt so alone among them, especially when he saw couples posing together with El Castillo in the background.

The pyramid—which was also known as the Temple of Kukulcán, the plumed serpent—was as large and impos- ing as he and Patricia had imagined it. He stared at the throne room at its top. A cool zephyr blew over the field.

She would have loved it. He could imagine her standing beside his lean frame, gawking at it without uttering a word, her silence a form of reverence. *My ancestors built this*, she might have thought. He could imagine her circling the pyramid, squinting at it, searching for the best angle before taking out her camera to snap a picture of it.

Brushing sweat from his eyebrows, Javier walked toward the pyramid. A few tourists milled around its base since climbing it was no longer permitted. The patches of clouds that had provided cover from the blazing sun had drifted on. The sweltering heat of the Yucatán became more unbearable. Javier marched on with his head bent, sweat running down his forehead and drenching his back. He was determined to get as close to it as he could. He had come so far.

When he approached the foot of the pyramid, Javier heard someone approach. Out of the corner of his eye, he saw a man wearing a baseball cap.

"Amigo, amigo . . . friend," the man said with a thick Spanish accent. He wore a worn T-shirt and khakis. "Do you like? Fifty pesos." The man held out a wooden replica of the pyramid. Javier frowned and waved him off.

As he stared at the pyramid, Javier couldn't help but wonder how it appeared during its construction. The Mayans had no wheel. The limestone used to build the colossal structure was hauled from quarries hundreds of meters away, past the jungle thicket that enveloped the ruins. He imagined the sweat that must have poured like rivulets over these fields. The lives and vitality lost—all expended to create this one object.

Javier unzipped the bag around his waist and took out the camera. It had been Patricia's—a Canon SLR camera she had owned long before they met, nine years before. The day prior to his flight to the Yucatán, he nearly decided to bring his digital camera instead because he was afraid he would become morose whenever he gazed through this one's lens. But when he awoke the next morning, he packed her camera. In a way, she would be with him when he would peer through the camera she had looked through for so many years. Her eyes could live through his on this trip to the Yucatán, one they had vowed to take.

Javier lifted his head to look up at El Castillo. The sun glared above its zenith. He squinted and lowered his gaze to the plateaus that divided the pyramid. He raised her camera and looked through the viewfinder only to realize that he had no interest in taking any pictures. It meant nothing without her to share it with.

Seven months before, during a heavy downpour, Javier drove his car up into their driveway. He left it there since Patricia always parked her car in their garage. One of her college friends was in town, which meant Patricia was bound to cook a delicious meal for their guest. *Her exquisite chicken curry to show off her cooking skills?* he wondered. *Or would it be the creamy peanut butter chicken that his mother had taught them to make?* He licked his lips in anticipation. Once he stuffed his CD cases into his business bag, Javier flung the car door open and stepped out into the rain, holding the bag above his head. Cold droplets of rain sent a chill down his neck as he grinned and scurried into their house, his red tie flapping over his ear.

Inside, Javier was surprised to find that Patricia was

not home. He called out to her as he walked to their bedroom. Her shoes rested by their bedside. He checked his cell phone for any missed calls, but there were none. Confounded, he marched to the garage. Her car was not there. Nor any wet tire tracks. He figured she must have run a last-minute errand to the supermarket.

Back in the kitchen, he pulled out his cell phone. He thought about calling her, but then his phone rang. He stopped in the hallway where a portrait of them smiling in front of a waterfall, a bright purple flower pinned over Patricia's ear, hung facing the front door. It was an unidentified caller.

"Hello," he said.

"Is this Mr. Javier . . . Velasco?" the man asked, mispronouncing Javier's surname.

"It is."

Javier tensed up. His back tightened. The man's tone sounded grave.

"Mr. Velasco, I'm calling from the emergency room at Washington Hospital. Your wife, Patricia Velasco-Arroyo, has been in a vehicular accident."

"Oh my god, is she all right?" Javier said, staggering into their living room. "What happened?"

"They can share those details with you at the hospital."

"Is she all right? Can you at least tell me that?"

The man hesitated. "Sir, you need to come to the ER," he said.

Javier shut his phone and held it limply by his side. He glanced around the living room, the house they had forged together.

"Oh god, this can't be happening, this can't be happening," he mumbled to himself as he fell to his knees. He put his hands on the hardwood floor. His body trembled as he mumbled the same words over and over again. He curled on the ground and cried until his tears and drivel formed a pool around his mouth.

🍾

Standing along the pyramid's base, Javier squinted as he tried to make out the serpentine shadow cast along the northern staircase to coincide with the autumnal equinox. A tour group approached. The Mayans had constructed the pyramid to reflect the 365 days of their solar calendar: ninety-one steps on each of four staircases with the top platform counting as the final step. He had planned his trip to visit Chichén Itzá the day before the equinox. That's how Patricia would have planned it.

Javier remembered a performance he attended a few months before by the indigenous dance group Patricia was a member of. He had stood to the side of the school gymnasium, watching her group dance around their pot-bellied elder as he banged two sticks on the huehuetl, an upright tubular drum. Patricia dressed in her ances-tors' traditional regalia for those rehearsals: a skirt, san-dals, ayoyotes around her ankles, a colorful huipil for a blouse, and a feathered headdress. He often drove her to the school where they practiced so he could watch them dance. He would smile with pride when he watched Patricia hop and twirl and sing with her group, the gym-nasium echoing with their chants, their thunderous drumbeats, their rattling ayoyotes that Cortés was unable to silence.

Watching her dance group, Javier became obsessed with

the trip to the Yucatán they never made together. He became resolute on making the trip alone. He became certain that there was *something*—an epiphany, a moment of transcendence, of peace, or perhaps resolution—that awaited him at the ruins.

Walking from the pyramid, Javier passed a sunburned couple. A camera dangled from the woman's willowy neck as she strode in front of her partner. The man trudged behind, reading his guidebook aloud, explaining to her how the pyramid was built to reflect the Mayan calendar. A wave of emptiness seized Javier as he saw himself in this man's position. He imagined Patricia, camera in hand, crouching beside the pyramid to snap a picture of the gigantic serpent head at the bottom of the staircase.

He continued on to the dusty path to el cenote sagrado—the giant sinkhole where the Mayans tossed sacrificial offerings to their gods centuries before. He tried to hold his head high beneath the sun that beat down on him. Along the path, rows of indigenous vendors gathered beneath rows of ceiba and palm trees. They placed wooden statues of Mayan soldiers, engravings of serpents, and plates with festive village scenes on top of colorful blankets. Others sold earrings, jade necklaces, or rings that glimmered in the sunlight. When he drew near, their conversations meshed into an indistinguishable, droning murmur. He averted his eyes and prayed that none of them would approach him. He wished no one was around. This trek to the sacred cenote was supposed to have been taken with Patricia. He could not let go of that fact.

†

Right after the accident Javier considered every factor that could have contributed to it. It was his worthless attempt to see if it could have been avoided had one miniscule variable changed. The key fact was that it had rained that day. Patricia's car had hydroplaned on the slick concrete when she drove on a curving road—one she drove every day to work. She lost control of the car and slammed into a light pole—all its force unleashed onto the front of the car. Her neck snapped, the neck that had a ticklish spot at its base that he loved to kiss while they lay together in bed.

The police report estimated that she had been traveling thirty-eight miles per hour at the point of contact, which was only three miles over the posted speed limit. Her friend's arrival and their dinner plans had not rushed Patricia, he deduced. According to eyewitnesses, no one had cut her off or done anything to force her to jerk the steering wheel. The tires on Patricia's car were practically brand new, which he verified with an invoice she had kept. And the brakes were in good shape. She had driven her car for years without incident. Javier could not understand why this had happened—why it seemed as if, no matter what, it was her time. Their end.

A few days after the accident, he drove to the spot where she had died. He parked his BMW to the side of the road. The dark-gray sky above felt like it was meant to oppress him. His heart began to beat faster as he waited at the sidewalk for all the vehicles to pass. Once it was clear, he scurried out onto the street where the police report stated her car spun out of control. He inspected the ground for any oil, any slick substance, *anything* that could begin to explain how and why this had happened. His eyes frantically combed over the pavement for anything out of the ordinary, but he found nothing. Then an oncoming diesel startled him with a booming honk. It took Javier a second before he decided to step out of its way. The truck honked again, this time longer. As he trudged back to his car, the truck driver leaned out the window and shouted, "What are you, fucking *sleepwalking*?"

At night Javier would often turn from side to side, his sleep fleeting, evasive. He had thought about the accident so much, and he wished it was due to someone's reckless negligence. He wished it could have been a drunk driver who struck her car, causing it to spin out of control and crumple into the pole. He wished it was a defective front strut that the manufacturer knew could give out at any moment. He wanted it to be something as simple as that so he could have something to direct all his anger and anguish toward. But it wasn't so, and he was left in the deafening silence of their house with one question and no answer.

After he sat on a rock and drank from his bottle of water, Javier rose and wiped the dust off his shorts. He swung his backpack onto his damp shirt and felt a rush of cold run down his back. He stared ahead at the stream of tourists trudging down the long path to the cenote. The sun was merciless, his mouth parched, his head light from fatigue.

Javier kept to the middle to pass the tourists who slowed to glance at all the novelties the vendors sold. The path was not smooth or even, teeming with dips and jutting rocks. Javier pushed on for what seemed a minute eternity until he reached the cenote.

Before him, like a crescent moon, a crowd of people gathered around its perimeter. The sinkhole was wider than a hockey rink. Javier took out his bottle of water and swallowed the last mouthful as he crept to its edge. The cenote was about a three-story descent if one were to slip and fall in. Its subterranean water was a dense green. He stared and stared at it, searching for any movement, any sign of life bubbling beneath its surface. After he saw none, he turned his attention to the sinkhole's craggy limestone walls. They were steep and high. With no mounting gear, he could not imagine how someone could climb out of the murky pool.

Once Javier stepped away from the edge, he heard a park employee shout at a young man who had thrown a rock into the cenote. Javier turned back to gaze at the water's surface. The ripples from the splash parted out toward the limestone walls in perfect circles. The sight mesmerized him. His thoughts drifted to all the gold necklaces, jade idols, animals, and people the Mayans had thrown into the pool as sacrifices for their rain god. They believed cenotes were portals to the afterworld. Javier stared into the green, opaque water and swore he saw a few bubbles surface.

When he snapped out of his spell, Javier walked over

to the nearby gift shop. A few tourists stood beneath a cooling fan, waiting for the bathroom to free up. Javier waited his turn, then he urinated in the cramped room before stepping to the sink. He removed the ring from his pinky finger and placed it to the side. He kept his wedding ring on and splashed water over his sweaty face. Since Patricia's death he had never removed it. The mere thought of losing it would twist a knot in his stomach.

Back out in the shop, Javier realized he had left his pinky ring in the bathroom. He could feel it missing from his hand. Patricia had given it to him years before on a trip to Spain. He darted back to the bathroom, knocked on the door, and heard no response. He opened the door. He gasped when he found a majestic Indian headdress resting on the sink, facing him. It was decorated with long, striped, pointy feathers in brilliant shades of red, yellow, green, and turquoise. Each feather was three-feet tall—about half the size of his body. They looked especially large in the small bathroom. His mouth agape, Javier carefully approached it. At the base of the headdress lay a beautiful jade necklace. The pieces were finely carved and elongated to resemble the fangs of a jaguar. On the floor was the rest of the regalia: sandals, ayoyotes, gold armbands, and a decorated taparrabo—a loincloth to wrap around his waist. Javier lifted an ankle shaker and shook it. It rattled loudly, echoing off the bathroom walls. He shook it again, this time longer as he tried to make sense of it all—how all this attire had suddenly manifested. He took a deep breath. He closed his eyes and massaged his eyelids before he exhaled. When he opened them again, the headdress and regalia were still there.

After he ran a finger along a quetzal feather, Javier understood what he must do.

He put the headdress on. It fit snugly, the tops of the feathers bending along the ceiling. He sat on the toilet and removed his shoes, socks, and shorts, discarding them in a corner along with his backpack. Javier slipped his feet into the sandals and tied their ropes, just like Patricia had many times before. He stood and wrapped the belt tight around his waist before he pulled the bracelets and shakers over his wrists and ankles. He gave a few kicks to hear the ayoyotes rattle. Javier took a profound breath. He felt a weight lift within him.

The people gathered at the cenote that afternoon will never forget that day. Somewhere in their respective memories is the sound of those rattling ayoyotes, that flurry of footsteps. For some folks gathered at the cenote that day, any sound resembling that rattle can conjure the vision of a man running toward the cenote before flying off its edge, his arms outstretched, feathers from his headdress fluttering in the air like fallen leaves as his body, a blur of golden brown, dove headfirst into the pool. A hush came over the crowd as they scampered to the mouth of the cenote to peer down. His splash created perfect circular ripples, one after another, spreading out to the limestone walls before dissipating. The crowd stood and waited. They began to whisper to each other.

"Did you see him?"

"Are you sure it was a man?"

"It's probably one of the locals, pulling a stunt to get some money from us. He'll come back up in a minute after he's given us a scare."

Feathers from his headdress floated atop the cenote's green water, but Javier never resurfaced.

PAINT IT CHANTREA

Diego stirred about his bedroom for a good long while, trying to decide whether he should wear a long-sleeve button-down shirt that Jorani would probably like on him or a T-shirt with a cartoon owl that said, "Give a hoot. Don't pollute!" which her daughter, Chantrea, might think was cool. He figured Chantrea was the one that he had to win over. While he took turns putting the shirts on to look at himself in the mirror, it seemed like a crucial decision with vast potential ramifications. Once he chose the button-down shirt, his armpits were already damp.

When he knocked at Jorani's apartment, her nine-year-old daughter opened the door. Her straight black hair hung down her back. She had dark, penetrating eyes.

"Hi, Chantrea," Diego said. "How are you?"

"I'm fine," she said, holding the door for him. Chantrea closed it and darted to her bedroom, shutting the door behind her. Jorani greeted him with a hug and a peck on the lips. She glanced at his pressed shirt, blue jeans, and Oxford shoes.

"You look nice," she said with her thick Khmer accent. "You look like a young school teacher."

Diego blushed.

"You don't look too shabby yourself," he said. She wore a red blouse and tight-fitting jeans that showed her figure well. Diego peered around the living room.

"Take a seat." Jorani led him to the dining table, which was already set. "Dinner's just about done."

He sat at the table. He gazed at the family portraits hanging on the wall. Before long, Jorani called her daughter to join them. She carried two plates of amok to the table. Each one held bowls made of large green leaves filled with steaming rice and a curry of diced fish and vegetables.

"Oh wow, this looks great," he said. "Can I help with anything?"

"Nope, you're our guest," Jorani said, bringing back one last plate with a smaller bowl, which she set at the head of the table. "Chantrea! Dinner's ready!"

Chantrea's bedroom door squeaked opened. She marched to her chair and stared at her bowl.

"Thank you for having me over for dinner," Diego said.

They took a bite. He grinned. "This is really good, Jorani. I think I'll ask you for your recipe."

She nodded. Diego looked over at Chantrea. "So how was school today?" he asked.

"It was fine," she said, continuing to stare at her plate.

"Tomorrow's Friday. Are you looking forward to the weekend? Any plans with your mom?"

"Not that I know of. She's probably dropping me off at my aunt's house again."

Diego glanced across the table at Jorani. She wiped her mouth with a napkin.

"Chantrea, if you don't want to go over to Aunt Mealea's, you don't have to. I'm not trying to force you."

Chantrea stuffed a spoonful of rice and curry into her mouth. The three ate quietly.

"Do you have a favorite subject at school?" Diego asked.

Once Chantrea finished chewing her food, she glanced in his direction. "Science." Without pause, she shoved another spoonful into her mouth.

"You like math too, right sweetie?" Jorani said. "She's always getting the highest score in class."

"That's terrific. I'm not so bright when it comes to math, but it's important to be good at it. Do you think you'll be a scientist like your mom when you grow up?"

"Maybe."

The silence unsettled him. He could practically hear each of them chewing their food.

"Chantrea *loves* animals. She loves the Oakland Zoo. Have you been there?"

"Yeah. Me and Oscar have gone there a couple times. Maybe we can all go sometime?"

Jorani turned to her daughter. "We can take your cousin, Michelle, too."

"Why are you saying *my cousin*, Michelle? I *know* she's my cousin."

"Sweetie, I am saying that for our guest, who has never met your cousin and doesn't know her name."

"Guest? He's your boyfriend, mahk."

Diego nearly choked on his food. He grabbed his napkin to wipe his mouth.

"Chantrea, I know this is all new for you, too, but Diego and I are dating. He is not my boyfriend. Maybe someday he and I will decide if we would like that. But right now, we're still trying to get to know each other."

"Well, I can tell that's what *you* want," Chantrea said. She set her spoon down. "I'm not feeling hungry. Can I go to my room?"

Jorani sighed. "You're excused. Remember, it's your turn to do the dishes."

With an icy silence Chantrea took her bowl and placed it in the sink. She hastened over to her bedroom and shut the door. Jorani grimaced a smile at Diego. He nodded understandingly. They finished their dinner, struggling to converse freely. Although Chantrea's door was closed, he felt like their conversation was being monitored.

Soon afterward, he hugged Jorani good-bye. He hung his head as he walked from her apartment. He was unsure if he should ever come back.

Diego met them at Bill E. Beaver's when he accompanied his nephew, Oscar, to a kid's birthday party. He was completing a perfect bonus round on *Galaga* when the unmistakable intro to the Rolling Stones's "Paint It Black" caught his attention. He whipped his head in the song's direction as a whirlwind of scamps dashed through the arcade. That's when he first saw Chantrea. Her back was to him, a toy guitar in her hands. Her shoulders were slumped with bored indifference as she hit each note, the *Guitar Hero* crowd cheering her on. She wore teeny black Chuck Taylors, jeans, and a blue cardigan. *How curious*, he thought. *What young girl in this text-message, Hannah Montana age would play that anguished 1966 song on* Guitar Hero, *let alone at a children's party?*

When the kids and parental units were summoned to the dining room, Diego and Oscar strode in like victors. Oscar wore the Bill E. Beaver flip watch he and Diego had earned with all the tickets they won. He showed it off to his friends, including Chantrea. She laughed at the plastic whiskers that were used to flip it open.

"I'm sure a real rodent wouldn't appreciate that," she said. "You can mess up a cat's sense of balance by cutting their whiskers."

"Is that true, Uncle Diego?" Oscar asked, peering up at him with a scrunched face.

"That's what I've heard," he said. He tried to hide a look of puzzlement as he wondered why a nine-year-old would know that, let alone associate that with the plastic whiskers of a beaver-faced watch.

Diego followed Oscar and Chantrea over to a table where Jorani sat. She had a dark-brown complexion, thin eyebrows, and a fit build. He figured she must be his age—in her early thirties. He and Oscar took a seat across from them. They exchanged greetings.

"Is that your son?" she asked.

"No," Diego said, giving a chuckle. "I'm his uncle. Your *favorite* uncle, right Oscar?" He nudged his nephew in the side with his elbow. Oscar flashed a missing-tooth smile.

"What do you do?" she asked him.

"I write grant proposals for a nonprofit that works toward bringing literacy to impoverished children. And I tutor some kids on the side. I used to be a teacher. How about you?"

"I work at the pathology lab for UCSF."

Inside, Diego had to fan and cool himself. He had a serious weakness for studious-nerdy types.

Soon after, the aroma of melted cheese and pepperoni wafted in the air as a factory line of pizzas was brought into the room. In short time Diego found out that Jorani was born and raised in Sihanoukville, a small beachside town in Cambodia. He was thrilled to tell her he had visited it four years before on a trip to Southeast Asia. He was surprised to find that her fellow Khmers reminded him of his South American family: warm, generous, laid-back, and adept at laughing away life's difficulties. As he told her this, Jorani smiled and tilted her head to the side, running her hand through her hair.

Diego noticed she didn't have a wedding ring. He had never gone out with a single mother. In fact, he had not dated much at all in the past two years since he overcame a battle with leukemia. The last woman he had dated stopped returning his calls once he told her he was a recent survivor. He was damaged goods. And though it hurt to be dumped, he couldn't blame her. No one knew if he would get sick again.

As they ate their pizza, Oscar folded a prize ticket into a small triangle. He held it against the table with his index finger and reared back the middle finger of his right hand. Chantrea made two Ls with her hands as Oscar flicked the paper football and it twirled over.

"Good one!" Diego said. He turned to Jorani. "I taught him how to do that."

After the kids finished playing paper football, Diego noticed how aloof Chantrea was compared to the other kids. Her eyes scanned the room while she took a sip from her cup, as if she was sizing them all up.

"Ray's dad didn't show up again," Chantrea said to

Oscar. "I've *never* seen him. I bet you his parents divorced and he's just too embarrassed to tell anyone."

Jorani became quiet after Chantrea said this.

A lanky teenage employee walked into the room. He held a big chocolate cake with one lit candle.

"Oh man, I'm *stuffed*," Diego said, patting his belly.

"Me too," Oscar said, mimicking his uncle's tummy patting.

After they sang to birthday boy Bobby, the smiley birthday cake entourage of Bill E. Beaver and Shelly Squirrel lumbered into the room. Each mascot held an assortment of balloons. "Billy! Billy!" the kids chanted before rushing over to them. Diego smirked as he watched them swarm the mascots like a cloud of locusts.

"Let's go get a balloon!" Oscar said to Chantrea.

"What do you want a stupid balloon for?" she said.

Oscar hesitated, then he scampered over to the mascots. Chantrea stared across the table at Diego as he conversed with her mother.

"I saw you playing 'Paint It Black,'" Diego said to Chantrea. "I love that song."

She crossed her arms. She stared at him with a yeah-so-what expression.

"Sweetie," Jorani said, leaning toward her daughter, "it's rude not to respond."

Chantrea sighed. "It's a good song," she said with the kind of excitement reserved for eating a rice cake.

"Where did you get such good taste in music?" he asked her.

"My mom."

"They play a lot of Stones in Cambodia," Jorani said. "It was the only good thing that came out of that war . . . all that rock 'n' roll we got from the Americans."

Diego smiled and nodded. Chantrea rolled her eyes. She ran off to join the kids.

Suddenly, the Bill E. Beaver mascot howled in pain just as a cluster of balloons floated to the ceiling. Giggling, Chantrea ran past Jorani and Diego into the game room. They looked at each other with befuddlement. Oscar scurried over to their table.

"What happened?" Diego asked.

"Chantrea yelled 'Human!' and kicked Bill E. Beaver in the shin!"

"Chantrea!" Jorani said, stomping after her daughter.

Diego couldn't help but laugh as the boys gathered around Bill E. Beaver and leapt to grab the balloons from his hand. *The force is potent with Chantrea*, he thought.

$$\dagger$$

A few days after the disastrous date at Jorani's apartment, Diego flipped through the newspaper at the home of his sister, Lorena. She packed Oscar's lunch box in the kitchen while he sat at their dining table. Meanwhile, Oscar trotted around the living room holding a miniature jet at eye level. He made a whirring sound that increased in volume whenever he tilted the plane to make a turn around the leather couch.

"That's strange," Diego said aloud. "An eastern Pennsylvania man was charged with trespassing after he allegedly broke into a home, cut his hair, and prepared fried chicken before being discovered."

He set the paper down as Oscar swooped around the couch with his arms out like a plane.

"Uncle Diego, what's the meaning of life?" he asked.

"Holy smokes, little partner. That's a big question. Why do you ask?"

"Today at school Chantrea told me there isn't one . . . that people make one up because they need to feel like they're important."

Diego tittered. He was not surprised that Chantrea—the girl who could probably play "Paint It Black" with the plastic guitar behind her head—had already figured that out.

"You wanna know what I think?"

"Yeah!"

"Diego," Lorena said, her hands on her plump hips, her face scrunched in the same frown she'd had since they were kids. Diego leaned toward Oscar in a conspiratorial fashion.

"Well, I think your friend is right. But, I do think that while we're here on planet Earth, that we should try to be happy without hurting others. Seems simple, huh?"

Oscar nodded.

"Just what other crazy things has Chantrea told you?" Lorena asked her son.

He tossed his plane up into the air and caught it.

"She told me her dad visits her in her sleep. She can't understand what he's saying because his voice is soft. And sometimes he carries his head around like the Headless Horseman!"

If life had become a *Ren and Stimpy* cartoon, Diego's eyes would have bulged and shot out of their sockets.

"Pretty cool, huh?" Oscar said.

On their first date sans kiddos, Diego and Jorani hit up

the Ruby Room, a dark, cavernous bar by the lake. A hard-rock song from Van Halen played from the jukebox as they sat at the bar. A few stools away, two hipsters drank cans of Hamm's.

"So how old were you when you had Chantrea?" Diego asked, nursing a beer.

"Oh, a crafty question. You're trying to figure out how old I am, huh?"

"Maybe I am."

She raised an eyebrow. "I was twenty-three. Twenty-one when I got married to Chantrea's dad."

Diego was startled she had introduced the subject of Chantrea's father so willingly.

"And what was he like? How did you two meet?"

Jorani told him she met her husband, Nimol, at the university they attended in Phnom Penh. He was a brilliant mathematician who aspired to be a professor like his father. After her sister and her husband moved to the San Francisco Bay Area, Jorani and Nimol intended to follow them. America seemed like a land with bountiful opportunities. But more importantly it was a land free of the ghosts and nightmares from their homeland, a country that was still littered with land mines that killed and maimed people, including children who were born decades after the war.

"Nimol's parents didn't survive," Jorani said. "Intellectuals like them were rounded up and killed after the Khmer Rouge took power. He was a child, just seven, when they found them. He never saw his parents again."

She paused, stirring the straw in her screwdriver. Diego wondered why she kept referring to him in the past tense.

"They put him in a labor camp. He survived *three years* in those death camps. Can you imagine?"

Hanging his head, he took a sip from his beer. "Were you in the death camps? I've read about them. When I was in Phnom Penh, I went to the Killing Fields."

"My family fled to Thailand right after the Khmer Rouge took power. We returned to Sihanoukville years after the Vietnamese overthrew them."

Jorani stared off, stirring her drink again. "Nimol was a gentle person, but he had terrible mood swings. We thought he'd get better once we left Cambodia, but it got worse once we got here. He found this country to be cold. Neighbors hardly knew one another."

"What happened to him?"

Jorani took a breath. "He killed himself."

"Oh, god." Diego put his hand on her shoulder. "I'm so sorry to hear that."

They sat with a wall of silence between them.

"I don't know why I told you. I *just* met you."

Jorani drank. He looked at her with a morose expression. "I can only imagine how difficult that must be," he said.

"Chantrea thinks her dad died from the war, which is essentially true, but—"

"That's understandable. I don't think that's something you would want to tell a child that young."

The two stared at the shelf full of bottles behind the counter. An '80s dance song played from the jukebox.

"Two years ago, I almost died," Diego said. "I had leukemia. I'm not telling you because it compares to what you've been through, but I figured I should tell you at some point and this seems as good a time as any."

"But you're okay now?"

"So far, so good," he said, knocking on the bar counter. "My doctors don't consider me cured until I've gone five years without relapsing, so I've got three more years of crossing all my digits."

Jorani gave a faint smile. The dim red lighting softened her face. "Well no wonder," she said.

"No wonder what?"

"No wonder I've trusted you with what I just said. You're different."

"I guess so. I *have* stared death in the face!"

Jorani held her drink up. They clanged their glasses. She stared into his eyes as she tipped her drink back.

"Chantrea doesn't seem to like me, huh?" Diego said.

Jorani laughed. "She's like that with most people. It takes her a while to warm to anyone. Plus, she's not used to having a guy around. It's still new to her. I haven't dated in a few years. But *this* is new for you, too, right? Dating a single mother?"

"That's also true. But how did you know?"

"I can tell. I wasn't—as you Americans say—born yesterday."

A drink later, they strolled over to the lake. It was a good night for a walk—brisk but not chilly for a late winter evening. A near full moon hung in the sky. Side by side, Diego and Jorani stared at the watery reflection of the lights that circled the lake like a ribbon of phosphorescent stars. They sat on a bench to watch the moonlight twinkle on the water. He reached out to her. Hand in hand, they watched a night heron fly over the lake as it cawed into the dark.

One night, Diego dreamt of Cambodia. It was dark. A full

moon hovered over a misty field of rice paddies. The palm trees shimmered a milky glow. Like a film camera, he watched a young Khmer boy hiding amid the rice stalks. The boy was covered in mud. It was Nimol. His eyes peeked over the stalks. A pair of yellow headlights from a transport truck pierced through the mist. Soldiers dressed in black with red scarves jumped out from the back of the truck. They barked at a group of blindfolded villagers, prodding them over to a ditch using the butt of their rifles. One of the soldiers instructed them to kneel.

The boy stared at a blindfolded woman. Her arms were skin and bone. A soldier stood behind her, holding a shovel over his shoulder. The villagers beside her quivered and murmured prayers to themselves. The soldier raised the shovel over his head. The boy buried his face in his hands. One by one, he heard the dull thud on their skulls and the sound of their bodies tumbling into the ditch.

The dream cut to a wide shot back in the paddy. Diego found himself wading in shin-high water, his bare feet digging into the cold mud. The boy slogged through the rice stalks before he ran toward him. "No, no, no! They'll see us!" Diego tried to shout, but the boy was propelled through the air as a land mine exploded. The boy screamed, splashing into the paddy's water. Diego dashed over to him. The soldiers spotted him and shouted.

When Diego looked down at the boy, he had turned into Chantrea.

🍶

Diego called Jorani the next day, and they began to see each other more regularly. One evening she came over to his apartment for homemade estofado de pollo, a Peruvian dish he had learned to cook from his mother. Another day he treated Jorani and the kids to ice-cream sundaes at Fentons Creamery. Afterward they flicked and chased a Frisbee around the playground by the lake. This romp in the sun got Chantrea smiling since she delighted in tossing the Frisbee out of Diego's reach so he could chase it down and flip it back to her with a smooth descent. They lost themselves in play.

Soon after, Diego and Oscar came over to Jorani's for a movie night. Diego brought his copy of *Lilo and Stitch*. Chantrea enjoyed Stitch's harebrained, destructive antics, but she got a real kick out of Diego's boisterous laughter, especially when the pint-sized alien stomped all over a miniature toy city. After the movie finished Diego perfectly imitated Stitch's voice by saying, "Ohana means family. Family means no one gets left behind." Chantrea laughed hard. "Can you do that again?" she asked, and Diego repeated the line in Stitch's voice. He grinned from ear to ear, incredulous that he had done something she actually liked.

The following week Diego surprised Jorani by showing up to her apartment to give Chantrea his hardcover copy of the *New Larousse Encyclopedia of Animal Life*. As he handed it to her, he explained that his parents had given it to him when he was a boy. He felt the book would be put to better use in her possession, especially since she loved animals. While Jorani stood beside her at the front door, Chantrea thanked him. Her mouth agape, she struggled to hold the hefty 640-page book in her arms.

Later, Jorani spent the night at his apartment. After they made love for the first time, they lay naked together. A candle flickered by the bedside. She ran her hands through his hair. He kissed the top of her head as she nestled against his chest. He tucked his arm beneath her warm body, staring at the flickering dance of light on the ceiling.

"Can I show you something?" Jorani said.

"Sure."

She sat up to reach for her phone on his nightstand. With her back against the headboard, she thumbed through her phone, its white incandescent light beaming through the dark. She handed him the phone. He stared at a black-and-white photograph of a young Khmer man.

"That's Nimol," she said. He had a high forehead and solemn, narrow eyes. He wore a black blazer and tie. "This photo was taken for the university where we studied."

"He was handsome," Diego said. "Chantrea has his eyes."

Jorani made a faint grin. "Everyone in my family has said the same."

He handed back the phone. "Thank you for showing me his picture. It means a lot to me."

"I don't want to feel like I'm hiding him."

They lay back down in bed, turned toward the candle.

"I think he would have liked you," she said.

He kissed her shoulder and pressed closer. After a while, he mustered the courage to ask her a question he could not put to rest. "How did he kill himself?"

Jorani stared into the flame. "He hung himself."

They lay silent for a long time.

One spring evening Diego cycled over to Jorani's apartment. Chantrea greeted him at the door. He was going to cook them a vegetable curry. After exchanging kisses with Jorani, he realized he had forgotten to bring a container of cream. He asked her if she had any in the fridge, but she didn't.

"Shoot," Diego said with Chantrea in earshot. "Is there a store nearby?"

"There's one three blocks over," Chantrea said.

"You wanna take him?" Jorani asked her.

To Diego's surprise, she agreed.

And so, Diego and Chantrea strode out into the residential streets. She took short and long strides to avoid stepping on cracks in the sidewalk. A black girl walked past them with a scraggly terrier. The dog's eyes were big like moons full of terror. The sun was beginning to set.

"Would you ever want a dog?" Diego asked.

"Yes."

"Like the one we just passed?"

"No. That dog looked like a wuss. I want a big dog. Like a German shepherd."

The neighborhood was quiet. They could hear their footsteps on the sidewalk. In the distance, a hip-hop song blared from a car.

"Even though you don't know it, I think we have a lot in common," Diego said in a soft voice as he stared at his shoes. "My dad's dead, too. He had a heart attack when I was twenty."

Chantrea stared at the pavement.

"I know I'm not family, but I want you to know that I'm here for you and your mom."

A convenience store stood on the corner of a main drag. Diego held the front door open for her. She followed him to the coolers, where he grabbed a carton of cream.

"You want anything?" he asked as they passed the candy aisle.

"No, thank you."

Back on the streets, Chantrea continued to step over the cracks in the sidewalk.

"You really like my mom, huh?" she said, staring up at him.

Diego nodded as they stepped through a pool of street-light. "I do, but I also happen to think you're pretty cool too."

"Why do you like us so much?"

He hesitated. "Because we're all survivors," he said. "Although your dad isn't with us, you come from him . . . and he went through *a lot* to bring you into this world. Someday, when you're older, you can read about what he went through."

"I already know."

Diego peered down at Chantrea. She stared ahead with a knowing gaze.

"And that's what makes you different from all the other kids. It's a curse and a blessing, but I think you already know that."

Before long they reached the apartment complex. He turned to look both ways before they crossed the street. Chantrea grabbed his hand.

"Here, I know a shortcut," she said.

DISASTER AT A WAKE

The sun descended over Arequipa as we rolled through traffic on our way to the mortuary. I sat in the passenger seat while my cousin, Luís, pulled his spotless silver Suzuki over to the curb behind a rusty, hulking bus that spewed plumes of smoke. My sister, Angelica, and mother rode in the back, wearing formal black dresses. The wake was for one of my mother's aunts, Tía Mecha. Although my sister and I hardly knew her, my mother asked that we accompany her. Some of our family would be there, she told us, including a distant uncle named Ignacio—a whip-smart bohemian who I reminded her of because we were both artistic.

We arrived, and a large sign above the doorway read, "Montesinos Mortuary." The building was made of white sillar adobe. Luís and I followed my mother and Angelica. Having just gotten off work, he wore blue jeans, workman boots, and a plaid button-down shirt beneath his mining company's forest-green jacket.

Luís stopped at the entrance. He pulled out his pack of cigarettes.

"Any cholitas in attendance?" he asked.

I leaned around him to peek inside.

"You know I only have eyes for the mamacitas," I said.

Luís and I were always trouble. When I was eighteen we used to get shit-faced at discotecas with our band of cousins, scoping for young arequipeñas to dance with. In front of my mother, at the lunch table or a family reunion, he would often rib me by asking if I wanted to go to San Tutis, which was code for the town whorehouse. Since our prior visit to Perú four years earlier, I had finally lost my virginity and begun to drink. Legally, that is. I had already awoken in my bed a few times without knowing how I got there. But I usually laughed it off.

The mortuary looked like it had once been a spacious house with two living rooms joined together. Burgundy couches lined the walls. I didn't recognize anyone who sat on them. They were all dressed in black and wore somber or expressionless faces. A few older men in black suits stared at me from a hallway that led to the back. I felt cramped in my tuxedo jacket as I stepped into the room. I spotted my Tía Inés and my grandmother. They sat near the open casket. Colorful sprays of flowers stood at its foot beside a kneeling pew for prayer. We exchanged hugs and hushed greetings. My grandmother wore her large, senior-citizen sunglasses along with a flowery bandanna. Weeks before, she had had an aneurysm removed. It left a bald spot on her scalp she didn't want people to see, but it just reminded me that she wouldn't be around forever.

Tía Inés was my grandmother's eldest daughter, the first of eight children. From an early age she was like a mother to all her siblings since my grandparents worked

61

long hours. At family reunions Tía Inés was always the one bossing people around: do this, do that. When we would reunite at a restaurant—twenty to thirty of us aunts and uncles and cousins at one table—she would stand next to the waiter and repeat every single food order given to them as though they were incapable of jotting it down correctly. At our fiestas she never danced or laughed with abandon like my other aunts or uncles; it's as if she was incapable of having fun, deprogrammed from feeling pure joy. We had clashed a few times. I'd gotten snappy with her when she'd tell me what to do like I was one of her kids.

My mother and Angelica took a seat on a couch next to the entrance. I sat on the armrest. We joined everyone gathered at the mortuary in quietly biding the time. That's what it seemed we were all doing.

As I glanced around the room, I remembered something my friend once told me. His psychology professor taught him that people have an unconscious desire to have sex in the face of death; it's like an unconscious denial of one's mortality. This theoretical stuff didn't interest me as much as the notion that cemeteries and mortuaries were teeming with living, breathing women who wanted to fuck. And so, I looked around the room as if I were a conquistador searching for gold.

And *there were* some gems in attendance: a cute girl about my age sitting in a corner; a few older women who were easy on the eye. After sitting solemnly for a few minutes, I excused myself. I stepped out to the front patio. Luís was exhaling from a cigarette.

"So," he said, "any mamitas in there?"

"Gimme a cigarette and I'll tell you," I said.

Luís handed me his pack. I leaned in and took a drag as he lit one.

"There's some gorgeous women in that room," I said, keeping my voice low as I peered inside. "Near the back is a flaquita sitting beside a woman who's probably her mom. She's a little on the young side. Probably not even twenty, but I bet you her conchita gets *so* wet!"

Luís doubled over to stifle his laughter.

"There's also a married woman. She's had her leg crossed away from her husband the entire time. She's just been looking off . . . up at the ceiling, up at anyone walking through the door. I bet you he's not taking care of business at home."

I inhaled from my cigarette and blew it off to the side.

"Now *this* one is the catch of the night." I nodded Luís over to the door. "Three o'clock. See the one sitting by herself, at the end of a couch?"

She was in her early forties—bronzed complexion, gorgeous face, sultry black dress that barely covered her knees, and a pair of black heels. I could have ogled her all night long, imagining how soft her legs felt to the touch, how I would kiss every inch of them like an apostle of her body.

"Look at her," I said. "She's wearing bright lipstick at *a wake*! See how she keeps wagging her leg? I'm telling you, she's itching for some fun! She's pent up about *something*."

Luís flicked his cigarette behind him. He patted me hard on the back. I smiled. He was the closest I had to an older brother. Too bad we lived thousands of miles apart.

Before long we heard a loud collision out on the street. Luís and I whipped our heads in its direction. A dingy brown car had crashed into the back of an old Volkswagen bug parked in front of the mortuary. The right side of the brown car reared up on the sidewalk.

A crowd gathered by the door. They gasped as they craned their heads to look at the wreckage. Luís scurried over to the crash along with a few other people. Once I caught up to him, a well-dressed woman in her late thirties ran to the cars. Her eyes bulged. She cupped her hands over her mouth. "Ignacio!" she shouted.

"Tío!" another woman yelled, dashing to the car.

Luís stepped out onto the busy street to the driver's side. The two women stood on the sidewalk a few feet from me. The younger one cried into the other woman's shoulder. I stepped closer. A man was slumped over the steering wheel. His arms were cradled around it, his head buried between them. I could hear his muffled cries. Then he raised his arm and pounded a fist against the dashboard.

"Oh, Ignacio," one of the women said. The eldest one ran around the back of the car. She tapped on the driver's side window as Luís stepped aside. All the cars and buses and minivans crammed with people slowed to stare at all the commotion.

"Ignacio. Ignacio," the woman said. She rapped the window as he continued to hit the dashboard. He raised his head and blinked his teary eyes as he turned to her. He was a slender man in his mid- to late fifties with a face cracked and weathered from too much sun and hard living. His mouth was agape. Trembling, he whipped his head around to gather his surroundings. He looked as if he had just come to after being knocked out. He gently opened the car door. He stumbled out with the help of the woman who stood beside him.

"Are you all right?" she asked, putting an arm around him.

"I'm fine," he said. "I'm sorry. Please forgive me. Please forgive me!"

As they walked from the wreckage, several more people joined us on the sidewalk.

"Ahh, it's Ignacio," a woman behind me said. "And he's drunk again."

"Typical," I heard my Tía Inés say.

They began to titter as a light-skinned man in his late forties stepped forward. His penetrating eyes looked over the damaged cars. A silence came over the crowd. The woman beside Ignacio stiffened when she saw him. Ignacio peered up.

"Nelson! Oh, Nelson," Ignacio said, like un chillón, a big crybaby. "Please forgive me, brother. Please forgive me!"

Nelson's face twisted with emotion as if he were on the brink of tears. "Don't worry about it," he said, putting a hand on Ignacio's shoulder. "Are you okay?"

"I had to run some errands, see some people. I began drinking early . . . and I drank too much. She was like a mother to me."

Ignacio buried his face into Nelson's shoulder.

"I know, Ignacio," Nelson said, patting him on the back. "We all deeply cared about her."

Ignacio staggered and took a step back. He hung his head. "I'm working right now, so don't you worry. I'll have your car fixed soon, I swear it."

"Hombre, I know you're good for your word."

With a stoic face, Nelson put his arm around Ignacio. They slowly made their way into the mortuary. A crowd by the entrance parted to allow them in, watching Ignacio be led in like an overgrown baby. Que vergüenza, carajo.

"So that's the Tío Ignacio I've heard about," I whispered to Luís.

"That's him. Although he just crashed into Tío Nelson's car, he's a good man. Tía Mecha practically raised him. Very quick-witted, but he's a madman. Too emotional for his own good. And he's a drunkard. Sometimes he drinks all day and all night. When he's like that, no one can control him."

Back in the mortuary, the room was quiet but humming with energy. It's as if the crash woke everyone up. No one sat idly. Everyone's attention was turned to Ignacio—the family fuckup.

He and Nelson trudged over to a pudgy, gray-haired man in his mid-seventies who sat on a mahogany chair by the foot of the casket. The old man wore a gray suit with dark sunglasses. He sat apart from everyone around him. He gently rose from his seat as Ignacio approached. My mother leaned to me.

"That's Tía Mecha's husband," she said.

Ignacio and Tía Mecha's widower embraced as I took a seat next to Angelica on the couch. They patted each other's backs and embraced for a long time. Everyone around them hung their heads or looked away. A few sobs broke out around the room as Ignacio stepped over to the casket. Tía Mecha's widower had held himself together until then. He slowly lifted his sunglasses to wipe away tears as Ignacio sobbed at the sight of his dead aunt. After a while he composed himself and patted the old man on the shoulder as he walked past him.

"What happened out there?" Angelica whispered into my ear.

"That guy who was just crying at the coffin plowed into the back of a parked car. He's our Tío Ignacio. He's totally wasted. Tía Mecha was his aunt. Like a mother to him, right, Mom?"

"Yes," she said. "Tía Mecha raised him since he was four years old, after his mother died of pneumonia."

A gentleman dressed in a black tuxedo extended a silver tray out to my cousin. The tray held a long row of cigarettes. Luís took one and thanked him. My jaw dropped.

"They're giving out cigarettes," I said, nudging Angelica.

"Wow," she said before our mother waved the attendant away.

Angelica waved him off as well. But I could hardly contain myself. I smiled at the gentleman as I took a cigarette.

"You need a light?" he asked.

"Please."

I nodded to him before he continued to circle the room. I took a drag and looked over at my mother. Her lips were pursed together.

"But it was free," I said as she shook her head.

I peered over at the foxy woman on the other side of the room. She slowly exhaled a long stream of smoke with an apathetic look on her face. As I sat there smoking my cigarette, I imagined myself bending her over the couch to work her from behind. My daydream came to a halt when Tía Inés's raised voice pierced the humdrum.

"Come on, Ignacio. No more," she said, her hands on

her hips, standing before Ignacio. He had apparently just grabbed a glass from another attendant who held a sliver tray stacked with what looked like rum and cokes.

"Mind your business," Ignacio slurred, his voice echoing off the adobe walls. Everyone stopped talking. They all looked over at Ignacio as he took a long sip from his drink while Tía Inés glared at him.

"You need to stop drinking. You've had enough."

"I said mind your goddamn business!"

A man stepped between them. He tried to drag Ignacio away.

"You have your own children and husband to order around like the dictator you are," Ignacio said, looking over the shoulder of the man who held him back.

A few people gasped. Ignacio glared back at Tía Inés, but it was like he wasn't quite there, like he was looking through her. My grandmother shuffled over to Tía's side.

"Don't talk to her like that, Ignacio," she said.

We all watched as Tía Inés glowered at him. He stood with his chest puffed out, his chin held high.

"Are you done?" she asked.

"Yeah. Done." Ignacio slammed back his drink then set it on a nearby table. He stumbled over to Nelson and put his hand on his shoulder.

"Brother, help me move my car off the sidewalk," Ignacio said. "I shouldn't get behind the wheel. We can go back to my house."

"Okay, Ignacio. Okay," Nelson said. His head drooped forward as they walked out of the mortuary, their footsteps echoing off the tiles.

"Malcriado," my grandmother hissed, waving her hand dismissively in Ignacio's direction. She looped her arm through Tía Inés's arm. They returned to their seats. Once the room became abuzz with chatter, I turned to Angelica with a mischievous grin.

"That was crazy, huh?"

"I know!"

I leaned back and took a long drag from my cigarette. My thoughts drifted to Ignacio, to the grimace he had when he left. I knew that expression. He hung his head the way I did after I crashed my car while driving drunk a month before. It was the same way I felt the morning after a night of binge drinking with my friends when I vaguely remembered calling my ex-girlfriend a "filthy bitch" for cracking a joke about the joys of lesbian sex. It was the same way I felt when I apologized to her the following morning. And she forgave me. She was a drunk, too, but she told me I scared her when I got like that because I'd get this far-off look in my eyes as if I was replaced by someone else, some awful guy who would say some jacked-up shit that my good side would have to apologize for the next day.

With nothing better to do, I glanced over at the woman that was driving me nuts. She looked back at me. I held my gaze long enough so she would know my glance was not accidental.

I walked outside. Out on the front patio, Luís was checking a message on his cell phone. The never-ending hum of traffic enveloped us. In the distance I could hear a boy chirping the destinations of his bus in a singsong, rapid-fire fashion—"Avenida Independencia Universidad Catolica Yanahuara Saga Falabella." I kicked a pebble toward the gate. Ignacio, Nelson, and two other men stood on the sidewalk, surveying the crumpled trunk of

Nelson's Volkswagen bug. I looked up to the orange sky, the sun setting over El Misti, the snow-capped volcano that loomed over the city.

"Lately I've been thinking that what I'd really like is to be buried in the ground," I said to Luís. "No coffin. No fancy clothes. Just dig a hole big enough to chuck my body in. We're no different than all the other animals. We all came from the earth, so why make it more complicated than that?"

"You really want to just be thrown in the ground? With no clothes?"

"Yeah, bro. Why do humans think they're more important than that? If my family doesn't want to see my rotting ass, they can just wrap me in a toga or something. But if they wouldn't mind burying me naked, I know I wouldn't, because you know what, I'll be dead!"

Then Luís and I heard the unmistakable sound of high heels clicking against pavement. My stomach knotted as I saw the woman sashay out with her cell phone in hand. As she walked past us, she raised the phone to her ear to answer a call. Her back to us, Luís and I beheld her figure. "Dios mío," I whispered.

"You've gotta talk to her!" Luís said.

"Are you kidding?"

"Ask her what plans she has tonight."

"She could be one of our *aunts*. She's too old for me."

"Tell her you're passing by, that you won't be in Arequipa much longer. Oh, she'll love that. And once she finds out you're an American, those legs will open far and wide, I'm telling you!"

The woman ended her call. She glanced at us as she flounced back into the mortuary.

"Well, you blew it, Miguelito. That was your chance."

"You know I had no shot. What would a woman like her do with a muchacho like me?"

"You may not know it, but *there are* women who like their meat young."

I smirked. "She's trouble. I can tell."

"But isn't that what you want?"

My eyes trailed off to Ignacio and Nelson. Nelson raised his arm, trying to flag a cab while Ignacio struggled to stand upright. My mother had told me about Ignacio a few times before. Told me he used to travel around Perú in a theater troupe when he was my age. He used to put on a puppet show in the town plazas. She told me I reminded her of him since I liked to write and videotape these silly fake commercials with my friends. She told me I had a mischievous smile just like his. Even laughed loud like him.

I stared at Ignacio, teetering behind his mashed-up car as Nelson helped to steady him.

"I just want to get out of here," I said, hanging my head. "I just want to go home."

MY AFTERNOON
WITH JESÚS

I was alone at my parents' house, sauntering about in my chonies with a beer bottle in hand. They were at work, and I had just called my employer to inform them I was quitting. My stint as a security guard was officially over. I had landed my first desk job—a profession that was, I supposed, more befitting of the college pedigree I had just earned. A celebration was in order for this rite of passage into a lifetime of white-collar servitude, that first step on a road that could lead to a house of my own someday (if I managed to live long enough to pay off the mortgage), a widescreen plasma TV, a 401(k), an orgy of a wedding, and devout reverence for the weekends (TGIF!). I moved back to my parents' to save up money and had returned to my suburban hometown, which felt infinitely tragic and dying compared to life in the city. In short time, one, two, three bottles of beer were drained for this momentous occasion. My buzz was good. The liquor store down the street called like a siren; my booze supply needed immediate replenishing. It was not even one o'clock on a Tuesday afternoon.

Jesús, a pandillero who lived at the end of the street, was pulling his green Chevy El Camino up his parents' driveway. Like always, he wore red attire: a crimson shirt with white Dickies pants and red sneakers. We had attended the same schools since we were kids. He was a year younger than me, the same grade as my sister. We exchanged nods as I walked by. His was a bit slower, head cocked back as though he were saying, "Qué onda, vato." Mine was quicker, less dramatic—more of a "¿Qué tal?" or howdy.

At the liquor store I saw Sam's Chevy Blazer in its usual spot right next to the dumpster. The sun glared off its black finish. It saddened me to see it. Poor Sam was always working at his store. Since I moved back home two months before—the college dorm-room phase of my life in the rear window—I drove by and saw his Blazer there almost every day, sitting like a dead weight. Most of the time, day or night, I was the only other person in there with him. (I don't like to refer to myself as a "customer.")

Sam stood behind the counter. He was a tall, imposing, big-bellied pervert with thick-framed glasses and a balding head. His greasy black locks pasted into a comb-over that could probably weather a hurricane. Whenever I proceeded to the register to pay for my booze, he often inquired about "all the tail" he seemed to think—or hoped—that I was "nailing."

He started in when I set my six-pack of Bass on the counter.

"My friend, how are you?" he said. He shook my hand. He had a firm, proud handshake that could crush a weaker man's hand. He smiled as though he were my grandfather. "Shit, man, you starting already?"

"Yeah. I've already got a few under my belt," I slurred.

"What's going on? You got that girlfriend of yours, the one with pink hair, back at your place? You two getting some afternoon exercise?"

He reached over the counter and playfully nudged my shoulder.

"Nah, man. We hit Splitsville. She was too crazy. And I'm already crazy enough, so it was no good."

"Oh, well. That's what your hand's for!"

"Good ole' righty!" I said, raising my right hand like a balladeer in the ecstatic throes of a sustained note.

I paid, said good-bye, and strutted out with a six-pack in hand. My fuck-it-all desire for beer was so overwhelming that I cracked open a bottle with the opener on my keychain once I stepped out. I took a hearty sip.

I drank on the way home. Before I knew it, I craved a cigarette. I considered going back to buy a pack, but then I'd be stuck with all those cigarettes when all I wanted was one for the stroll.

Jesús stood on the waist-high brick wall that separated his elevated front lawn from the sidewalk. It looked like he was waiting for someone.

"Hey bro, you got a smoke I can bum?" I said, peering up at him. "I'll give you a beer for one."

"Sorry bro, I don't smoke."

"Oh, you don't *smoke*, huh? Cough cough, hee hee."

Jesús smirked. He could tell I was loaded. He must have thought that was funny. A bit peculiar. From the time we went to grade school—back when my mom combed my hair to the sides like a good boy and dressed me in outfits that are grisly in retrospect—I had been antithetical to him. My sister and I got straight-A report

74

cards through junior high. We went off to college while Jesús and his younger sister stayed in our hometown, easing into a gangsta life. Not the dumping-bodies-in-the-marina type of life, but more of the tagging-their-turf-and-dealing-drugs kind. Because of this, perhaps he presumed I was a Peruvian choirboy of sorts. More at home with a textbook in my lap than a four-foot bong. But he would've been mistaken.

"Of course I toke. Sheeit," he said.

We were exchanging words! I couldn't believe it.

"By any chance, you got any on you?" I said. "I've been itching for some, but I don't have a hookup in this town."

"How much ya want?"

"Just enough for a joint. I'll take an eighth if that's the least you can sell. Roll one big enough for the both of us. I'll smoke us out."

"Aight. C'mon," Jesús said with a wave of his hand. He headed up the walkway to the front door. I tipped the bottle back, killed it, and set it on the curb. I excitedly pumped my fist. Six-pack in hand, I followed Jesús up to the creaky screen door, which was tattered and littered with a few dead moths. We stepped into a hallway.

"Wait here a sec," Jesús said. "Let's smoke in the back so my viejita won't give me shit."

He opened the first door on the right. It must have been his bedroom. The door was covered with an auto-graphed poster of a hot, bikini-clad Raiderette. Once he stepped out I followed him into a dim-lit living room that had all its curtains shut. A portrait of his familia antigua—his grandparents and their seven children, all solemn and serious—hung over the fireplace. Their ginormous television—the altar of suburbia—stood at the corner on the opposite wall. A leather chair and sofa faced it like ever-willing witnesses. My feet wanted to stop at their entertainment system to check out their shelves full of vinyl records, but Jesús opened the sliding door. He held the curtain open. The sunlight knifed through the room.

A flurry of barking startled me as I stepped out into the backyard. A boxer, tall enough to chomp out my intestines, was chained to a lemon tree by the side of the house. It scared the shit out of me even though it was out of mauling range. The dog—with the requisite spiked collar—lurched and snapped in my direction.

"Don't trip, I got him tied," Jesús said, as though he was explaining how to operate an electric can opener. "He ain't too friendly to people he doesn't know."

We walked to the narrow alley between his house and a wooden fence. Jesús held a blunt in his hand, a twamp in the other. He handed them to me along with a lighter.

"Thanks a lot, man," I said. "How much do I owe you?"

"Fifteen. It ain't the best," he said, nodding at the bag of weed, "but it'll get the job done."

"Hey hey, something's better than nothing most of the time."

With a flick of the lighter, I took a hit and passed it back. Jesús took a big rip. When he exhaled, the smoke seemed to roll out of his mouth like a factory chimney. I crossed my arms and chuckled in admiration. He handed it back. I sucked in a big hit—my attempt to join the big-boy league—but I ended up doubled over, coughing like a pack-a-day smoker who had just run up a flight of stairs. He laughed. After I coughed up a lung, I was feeling the sweet giggle.

I paid him before we finished the joint, then we walked through the side gate out to the front yard. Our neighborhood—the one I used to play hide-and-seek in when we were kids—looked new and hazy, vibrant not dead, beneath the sun. Everything felt a little make-pretend while I stared around with a tee-hee grin. When I turned to Jesús, I saw him standing on a pillar from the brick wall. He gazed down the street. The branches from the tree in his front lawn curled around him as though they were ready to embrace him, a child of the sun.

"Who you waiting for?" I asked.

"My homie's supposed to drop by and show me these new rims he got."

"For your ride?" I said, instead of "car" like I usually would.

"Yeah."

I walked over to his El Camino. On weeknights, past one or two in the morning, I've heard his car roll down our street. The hum of its engine is that distinct. Jesús can't be up to any good. Not in this town with jack shit to do at night.

"You got a nice fucking car, man," I said, running a finger along the green chrome that glistened as though it hummed with energy. "What kind of engine does it have?"

"220 horsepower."

"Nice," I said. "I'd like to get my own muscle car someday so I can pull up behind some slow-ass driver on Fairview Boulevard and rev the shit out of the engine!"

"People drive like pendejos here."

"They do! Like a bunch of old farts."

I stepped up to his lawn. I noticed that my hand felt light. "Ah shit, my beer," I said.

"Go through the gate. It's open."

My sixer rested by the fence where we had toked up. After I picked it up, I noticed the window on the side of the house. A white curtain with a beautiful embroidered floral trim—like the kind on huipiles—was parted halfway. I took a peek. Resting on the windowsill over the kitchen sink was a ceramic Olmec head. Beside it, seemingly ready to stiff-arm the head aside, was a silver and black figurine of Bo Jackson, who retired from football with a 5.4-yards-per-rush average—the highest in NFL history. It pleased me to know that his family were also Raiders fans. Beyond the windowsill was a round table with four chairs, just like in my parents' kitchen. And like our cocina, a morose painting of *The Last Supper*—the classic guilt-ridden, Latino Catholic touch—lorded over the table. It was then that I wondered if his parents played Trio Los Panchos, sentimental boleros, maybe even Marco Antonio Solís or Ricardo Montaner like my mother would during our family meals. Or did his old man play some oldies like "Suavecito"?

How did Jesús and I turn out so differently?

Out in the front yard, Jesús sat hunched over on the edge of the lawn. His legs hung over the brick wall. It looked like he was mugging for the entire world. I popped a beer open for him along with one for myself.

"Salud," I said, handing him a beer.

"Salud."

After we clinked our bottles and downed some beer, I stood on the lawn, unsure of what to do.

"Just sit and chill, brah," he said, nodding at a spot next to him.

"Thanks, man," I said as I took a seat. We stared out

past the street corner over to the main drag in the distance. My eyes followed a few cars as they drove down the street then a bus that appeared to be vacant as usual. After living in the city where people regularly took public transit, it pained me to see those empty buses driving around my hometown like phantoms cursed to circle the same route day after day, night after night. But I grinned and looked away toward something more pleasant, to the sunlight bending around the tree leaves above me. Just then, his sister came walking down the street.

"Oh shit," I said. My hand lurched over to the six-pack by my side. I was ready to hide it behind me.

"Don't trip. She don't give a shit."

We continued to look at her as she crossed the street. She wore one of those white T-shirts popular con La Raza and gangsta types—the Virgin Mary on the front, the Mexican flag beneath her. Her black hair was long and went straight down her back to her ass. Her baggy pants—surprisingly not red—obscured what must have been some fine legs.

"Whaddya think of my sister?" he asked.

I paused and chugged from my beer. Jesús looked in his sister's direction. Although I was inebriated, I had not forgotten that I was speaking with Jesús, a gangbanger. My posse—if I had one—hung out at bookstores and cafés, not on the streets. The heat we packed were pens and books, not gats and butterfly knives. Even through high school, when Jesús's crimson attire announced that he was a gangster of some level, he always struck me as an all right guy. A bit requisite macho, sure, but not fearsome or violent in spirit, though I'm sure he'd been in a brawl before. Or seen the glint from a switchblade.

"What do you mean?" I asked.

Jesús stared back at me. He made a pfffft sound. "Come on. Ya know what I mean."

It had been years since I'd seen her. Back in junior high she had chubby cheeks and a semi-butchy figure. Time had tightened those stout features into curves that could make a grown man weep. Maybe it was the black asphalt she walked on, refracting the sunlight around her, but she was bathed in light as though the sun was up to illuminate her at that moment. Her tits and hips looked godly, deserving of zealous worship. She was not a chiquita anymore.

"She's all right," I said.

"*All right?*" he asked.

"I mean, I wouldn't be disappointed if I had her in the back seat of my car, you know what I'm saying?"

He laughed and socked my shoulder.

"Ah bro, I was just fuckin' wit ya. My homies are always tryin' to get with her so I know, *I know*. Sheeit, sometimes *I* wish she wasn't my sister!"

We busted up. I would have never predicted that Jesús and I would *ever* have a conversation like this, let alone kick it in front of his house.

She walked by, staring at us with her brows furrowed. With my arms stretched behind me on the lawn, I twisted my head around. My eyes zeroed in on her sweet rear as she walked to the front door.

"Bendito diosito," I said, gritting my lips and making a cross over my forehead as though we were in church.

Jesús nearly fell off the lawn, doubled over in laughter. To my surprise she came to a stop. She turned back and shook her head with the faintest grin on her face. Could she have liked my compliment? Could I—a bohemian peruano who dug Zeppelin, Chopin, Parliament, and Whitesnake—ever score with a chola like her? Could that wet dream ever be fulfilled?

Not a minute later a car pulled up in front of Jesús's house. It was a red '67 Ford Mustang. It sparkled as though it had just floated down from the clouds upon a ray of sunshine. Jesús stepped over to the car. I followed suit with my six-pack in hand.

"Hey, see you later," I said.

"Take it easy, brah," Jesús said. He tried to slap my hand and fist-bump it in a way I was unfamiliar with, which left me grinning all embarrassed as I fumbled to reciprocate. I shook his hand instead.

After I passed a few houses I slowed down. I thought about hollering back to Jesús that we should kick it some-time and catch a Raider game. But even though my head was up in the clouds, I knew our paths had diverged a long time before, so I kept on going without turning back.

JUST ANOTHER DAY

On the train home from work, Miguel awoke to find a man sleeping beside him. The train car was packed. It had been half-empty when he boarded from the downtown station. He squinted from the sunlight streaming through the windows. It was always jolting to wake up to altered surroundings, as if much had changed in the fifteen minutes he napped.

As he turned his attention to the other passengers on the train, Miguel saw that many others were asleep. Men, women, suits, yuppies, laborers, vagrants, and students. Most of the people who were not asleep stared out at the passing landscape. He thought about all the time they passed away on the trains. All that time in this in-between space, replenishing their bodies with sleep—for time with their loved ones or another day at work. Now that he worked full-time at the library's resource desk, Miguel spent two hours every weekday on the trains, a yearly rate topping five hundred hours, or twenty entire days spent commuting. It saddened him to think of all those hours he'd never get back.

Miguel read his book for the rest of the ride to Fremont. By the time the train rolled to its final stop, a handful of people remained in the car. When he stood to walk off the train, Miguel noticed a gray-haired businessman with his head slumped against the window. The man sat two rows in front of him. He did not rouse when the train brusquely entered the station.

"Fremont . . . Fremont station. End of the line," the conductor said over the loud speaker in a singsong voice. "All passengers must off-board. This is now a Richmond-bound train."

Standing in the aisle, Miguel leaned over to tap the man's shoulder.

"Sir," he said. "It's the last stop."

The man did not move. Miguel tapped his shoulder again with more force. The man showed no sign of awakening. Miguel whipped his head to the train doors that would be closing soon. No one else was in the train car. He turned back to the man. A crumpled newspaper lay on his lap. A black leather briefcase rested by his legs.

"Doors are closing but will reopen," the conductor said.

Miguel leaned over to shake the man's shoulders. "Sir, wake up!"

The man's head slumped against the cold window-pane at an unnatural angle. Miguel's eyes bloomed.

"Oh god," he said, dropping his shoulder bag to the floor. The train doors closed with a "bing!" He bent close to the man's chest. It did not move. Miguel placed two fingers over the man's carotid artery just like he had learned two years before during a CPR training he took for one of his first jobs out of school. He felt no pulse. Reluctant to believe what he was witnessing, he grabbed the man's wrist to check for a pulse. There was none. He noticed that the man had no wedding ring on his hand.

His CPR training used rubber dummies, never a living being, so Miguel dashed to the end of the car. He pressed the intercom button. The conductor responded.

"Ma'am!" Miguel said. "There's a man in this car who won't wake up. He's slumped against the window and his chest isn't moving, and I checked for his pulse and I didn't feel any."

"You're absolutely sure there's no pulse?" she asked.

"There's none."

"Okay, just stay there and don't move him. I'm calling emergency medics. I'll be right there."

Miguel stared back at the man, his head angled against the window half a train car away. *Oh god, get me out of here*, Miguel thought while he walked back to retrieve his bag, careful to look away from the man. With his bag slung over his shoulder, he slouched forward on one of the seats next to the train doors. He stared out the window, past the parking lot where he could faintly hear sparrows chirping in a row of trees. Where was this man going? Did he have children he was leaving behind? Did he live alone like his father, who used to take this same train into the city for work?

Before long Miguel heard the station attendant's voice over the loud speakers. "Attention passengers. The Richmond train on platform one is out of service due to a medical emergency. *Do not* board that train. All passengers, please board the San Francisco Daly City–bound train, which should be here in nine minutes."

The conductor stepped through the sliding doors between the train cars. She strode over to the man. Miguel watched her study him. She grimaced and shook her head before stepping over to Miguel.

"You okay?" she asked.

"Yeah, I'm all right. I'm just, you know, sad for him. He looks young . . . like he's in his fifties at most. Younger than my dad."

She shrugged her shoulders. "We've all got to go some time."

As a crowd gathered on the platform, the conductor opened the train doors when the paramedics arrived. They pushed in a stretcher.

"Can I leave?" Miguel asked one of the paramedics. He had nowhere to be, but he wanted to be home in his apartment. It was beginning to feel like a long day.

"You can after one of the officers takes your statement," the paramedic said. "It shouldn't take long. Just procedure."

In a daze, Miguel stepped out onto the platform. A few bystanders stared at him before a BART police officer moved them aside. The station attendant's voice boomed again. Miguel stared off at the waning sun. Then he saw a man in a business suit pacing along the platform.

"Hey Bill, it's Paul," the man said in a loud, self-important voice. "Listen, I'm stuck at BART in Fremont. I'm going to be late because some guy fainted or had a heart attack or something. We might have to reschedule with their sales team."

Miguel inched in the man's direction.

"Yeah, yeah. Believe me, *I'm sorry*, too, but shit happens, right? Talk to you tomorrow."

The man snapped his Blackberry shut. While he stared at him, Miguel could imagine this man sitting behind an executive desk in an office perched above the city. He seemed like the kind of guy who spit out phrases like "Let's hit the ground running" or "I want 110% effort" or "These quarterly numbers are low, people." This was the kind of man his father used to grumble about when he came home from work, the kind of man who would walk past him every morning without acknowledging him, as though a lowly lobby attendant did not exist. Miguel glared at the businessman. He wanted to slug him. For once, he didn't want to bite his tongue to such a man, even if he was a stranger. He took a step toward him, planting his feet out wide.

"That guy you just talked about is *dead*," Miguel said. "Have some goddamn respect."

The businessman flinched and turned away.

"Asshole," Miguel muttered, glaring at the man's back before he walked over to the police officer.

After he gave his statement, Miguel began to descend the stairs. He stopped to peer into the train. The dead man rested on the stretcher, covered with a yellow blanket. Though he did not know the man—what he had and had not done in his life—he solemnly hung his head and left.

Out in the parking lot, emptying with a flux of cars, Miguel took out his phone to call his dad. He had not spoken to him in months.

"Hey, Dad," Miguel said, staring at a sparrow that swooped through the sky above. "How are you?"

THE RIGHT CANDIDATE

Ernesto Burro, a young man who looks more dashing than his surname would suggest, had finally landed himself a respectable job. A recent college graduate with a liberal studies degree, he got a temp-to-hire assignment with the customer service department of a plumbing parts distributor. No longer would he have to toil his youth away as a security officer, sitting and sitting and sitting while he waited to play foil to would-be burglars. Although he was sad that he would no longer be able to refer to himself as "The Last Frontier on Crime" to his girlfriend, Gail—or draw comics at work (and technically get paid for it!)—he was pleased to get his first desk job.

On his first day at Buddington Distributors, Ernesto showed up to work ten minutes early. Dressed in brand-new slacks, a brand-new button-down shirt, and black dress shoes, Ernesto sat in the lobby with a lunch bag on his lap. He felt like such a good boy in his new clothes. All dressed up like an important person. While he waited for the office manager, he stared at the gleaming white toilet perched atop a seven-foot-tall revolving pillar in the center of the lobby. Two spotlights shined upon it, illuminating it as though it were an almighty obelisk to cleanliness. After a few minutes, Ernesto stood to inspect the plaque at the foot of the pillar.

It read:

In memory of Salvatorre "Sal" Attardo
Our gentle founder, 1933–2004

Next to the plaque was a 1970s-era color picture of a balding, middle-aged man with robust muttonchops. Dressed in a suit, he sat on a toilet flashing a thumbs-up to the photographer. An empty warehouse filled the background.

As Ernesto returned to his seat, Mrs. Doris Banke, a lanky woman of Norwegian descent, strode in.

"Hi, Ernesto," she said with a sugary voice as she extended her hand. "We're so glad to have you here."

"I'm grateful to be here!"

Ernesto followed her past the front desk then past a row of cubicles to a small kitchen.

"This is our break room," she said, giving a sweeping wave of the room. "Feel free to bring in a lunch or snacks and store them in our fridge. Just make sure to label it or else our hungry warehouse pickers might consider it open season on leftovers! We have some handy-dandy sticky notes and markers over here."

Mrs. Banke showed him the time clock in the corner of the kitchen along with his own electronic badge in its alphabetic slot. She pointed at a bottle of hand sanitizer that rested on a shelf beside the time clock and instructed him to use it every time he returned from his breaks. On the rest of the office tour, Ernesto noticed hand sanitizers everywhere. At every cubicle. By the fax copier. Postage machine. Communal staplers. Office inboxes. By the back entrance to the warehouse. They even had one at each table in the break room. *What's up with that*, he thought. *Was Howard Hughes a founding member?* His staffing agency (and real head honcho) had told him that they labored to find "the right candidate" for Buddington Distributors.

Jeanene, a young, voluptuous black woman, worked the front desk overlooking the lobby. She was assigned to train Ernesto on their order-entry system. Throughout the morning she communicated things simply to him and kept a calm demeanor despite the heavy volume of incoming calls. She was a relaxing presence for the office in spite of her uncommon obsession with Pixy Stix. About every half hour, Jeanene reached into a jar beside her computer that was filled with those powdered candies. After tearing an end off, she would crane her head back and shotgun the entire stick.

"Sometimes I don't get enough sleep at night, so this is what keeps me energized," Jeanene said, bags beneath her eyes. "I don't drink coffee at work anymore. It's a diuretic."

And so, the morning came and passed. At midday Ernesto ate his brown-bag lunch and conversed with Jeanene in the break room.

"What's with all the hand sanitizers?" he asked. "Is it like this all the time, or is it just because winter's around the corner?"

"It's always been like this as long as I've worked here,"

she said. "The general manager's kind of a germaphobe. His office has its own separate side entrance."

Ernesto wrinkled his brow. He also found it curious that their vending machine was filled to the gills with multi-grain muffins but refrained from inquiring about it.

"How about the toilet in the lobby. Have you ever gotten hypnotized staring at it?"

"No, but when I'm bored I've sometimes dreamt about sitting on it and peeing and waving to everyone."

After they finished their lunch, Ernesto strode to the bathroom. The coffee he drank earlier had given his bowels a jolt.

While sitting on the toilet, Ernesto reminisced on the past weekend of copious celebratory fornication with Gail, his girlfriend of the past nine months. She was proud of Ernesto for "getting a real job," although she loved it when he used to come over to her apartment after his nighttime shifts dressed in his security-officer uniform, intent on "securing the premises." She was the one who pushed Ernesto to apply to staffing agencies for administrative work. A business major and enterprising assistant manager at a local Starbucks, Gail implemented two successful initiatives at her café: the discounted day-old pastry basket by the register and a weekly board games night that was popular among "dorks and old farts," as she put it. She was fond of Ernesto because he was handsome, educated, and enjoyed watching plays and going to museums. He wished she would take an interest in his security-officer-inspired comic strip, *10-4, Gung Ho*. The only time Gail expressed an interest in his sketching— she called it "doodling," which was better than "waste of time" as his dad had called it—was when she asked him to draw a naked portrait of her à la Kate Winslet in her all-time favorite movie, *Titanic*.

Once he washed his hands, Ernesto scurried back to the break room. To his chagrin he was a minute over his break. After he filed his electronic badge away, he squirted some hand sanitizer on his hands and power walked to his cubicle.

At his desk Ernesto alphabetized a stack of invoices. A few minutes after he returned from lunch, an extension lit up on his phone. It was Mrs. Banke.

"Hello, this is Ernesto."

"Hi, Ernesto, can I see you in my office for a minute?" she said in a breezy voice.

He walked to her office, which was eight feet away. Mrs. Banke's door was closed. He knocked. Through the heavy wood, he could hear her muffled voice tell him to come in.

Mrs. Banke greeted Ernesto with a big smile. She sat straight with impeccable posture. Ernesto could feel his buttocks clench. He grinned and sat at a chair opposite her. The room was quiet except for the soft hum of her computer.

"How is everything coming along?" she asked, her hands cupped on the desk.

"Fine so far. I'm not having much trouble figuring out the order-entry program."

"Good. We haven't overwhelmed you with too much work, too much info to process?"

"No, not at all. Well, not yet at least!"

"Ha ha ha, just you wait," she said with a turn of her head, swinging a fist in a get-one-for-the-gipper manner. "Now Ernesto, it's been brought to my attention that you clocked in a minute late from your lunch today. Is that correct?"

"Oh, yeah," he said in a my-goodness, what-was-I-thinking tone. "Before I came back in, I thought, you know, it'd be a good idea to go to the bathroom and wash my hands. I'm sorry for clocking in late."

"Oh, don't worry about that. A minute late . . . that's no biggie. However, it's a good opportunity to go over our toilet-room protocol."

Mrs. Banke rolled her chair up. She straightened herself again, her eyes penetrating into his. She gave a cheery smile that appeared to be forced. Ernesto dug his fingers into the underside of the chair.

"I'm not sure if your employers informed you, but we have a strict etiquette for our toilet facilities, and I'm sure you've noticed that we encourage all employees to have their hands constantly sterilized with the hand sanitizers we provide at each workspace."

"Yes, I've noticed. Jeanene has reminded me about that, too."

"Good, that's good. Now, has she told you we expect you, at the end of the day, to wipe your desk counter before you clock out, even if it means staying a minute or two later?"

"No, no she hasn't."

"Okay, well it's very important that you do. Every day."

"Sure. Absolutely," he said with vigorous nods. "Winter's just around the corner, and I'm sure you're just trying to cut down on germs."

"Precisely. Germs are *nasty* fellows. So insidious because they're invisible to our eyes. Now, we're being consistent with our toilet rooms as well, which is why we have disinfecting wipes on every toilet."

"Oh yeah, I noticed that, too. I thought—"

"They're for wiping down the toilet seats after *each* usage," she said in a lower register. "Didn't you read the sign over the toilet?"

"Sign?"

Ernesto felt his stomach turn. His question was a fib. He had noticed a sign but failed to read it in his haste.

"Well, I'll bring up this matter with our Restroom Committee. It was probably one of those miscreant warehouse workers who took it down. In the past they have drawn some rather heinous figurines on those notices."

Mrs. Banke peeled off a pink sticky note. She scrawled "Earl" on it and drew a thick X-mark over his name.

"Anywho! Did you happen to deposit excrement in our bathroom toilets today, during your lunch break?"

"Um . . . I did," Ernesto said. Mrs. Banke blankly stared at him. "I used one of the toilet seat covers. It, uh, covered the entire seat."

"That's good, but not good enough. But it's not your fault because you weren't told before. From now on, not only do you have to use one of the protective seat covers, but after you're done, *and after you've flushed the toilet*, you must take one of those wipes—which are disinfectants—and use it to thoroughly wipe the toilet seat. Why I'd even discourage you from using the bathroom to defecate altogether. I encourage you to do that at your own home because we are trying to crack down on germs, okay!"

"Ohhhkay. Don't worry. I'll make sure that happens."

He glanced at a picture by her monitor. He presumed it was her husband and their little boy. Those poor souls. She probably had a strict "Bathe Before Hanky" policy.

"I appreciate that, Ernesto. Now, the other reason we

do that is because all the toilets and pipes and sinks at this facility are our own. By wiping down the toilet seat cover—I know this may seem weird at first—we are paying reverence to our product. To our business, our work, *our livelihood*. You understand, right?"

"Yes, I do, completely."

After his first day at Buddington Distributors, Ernesto drove to Gail's apartment. Over takeout Chinese he told her about the toilet on the rotating pillar in the lobby; Jeanene's fixation—or addiction?—to Pixy Stix; Mrs. Banke's pep talk on eradicating butt germs; and the mysterious general manager who always kept his door closed.

"Well, that's an interesting management style," Gail said. "Instill corporate value by having your employees wipe their toilet seats after usage. That's fresh material, I'll say that."

Despite all the wackiness, Ernesto was still willing to work there. A job is a job. So the company was run by germaphobes. And they asked their employees to pay homage to their workmanship by wiping their toilet seats with disinfecting wipes. At least they didn't begin every workday by circling the toilet in the front lobby and bowing their foreheads to the linoleum floor as though it were a shrine. A job is a job is a job is a job.

The next morning, Mrs. Banke walked past Ernesto as he gathered facsimiles at the copier. They exchanged cordial grins like the ones he received from the office staff when he interviewed for the assignment a week before. Back then, Ernesto thought, *Gee, everyone here is so nice*, but now when the staff smiled at him in passing it felt different. It seemed as though they were trying to bottle something behind their tight-lipped grins.

Late in the day Ernesto went to the kitchen to refill his and Jeanene's cups with water. Two men in their early forties hovered around the coffeemaker. One of them was Mike, the sales manager, who he had met earlier. The other guy was one of the salesmen. Both had hearty waistlines.

"Whatcha doin' tonight, Lopez?" Mike said to his colleague. "Wanna grab some brewskies at TGI Fridays?"

"No can do, my friend," Lopez said. "I only go there *on* Fridays."

They laughed while Ernesto filled his cup at the water cooler.

"But really, I can't tonight. Meg and I are watching CSI at seven. Season premiere."

With both cups in hand, Ernesto turned to walk out of the kitchen.

"Made it through your second day, huh?" Mike said.

"Just about," Ernesto said.

"We got a potential rookie of the year right here," Mike said, nudging Lopez in the side.

"Hey, how many cups of water have you had today?" Lopez said to Ernesto. "You know we only allow office employees a daily total of six."

The men guffawed.

"But I can tell you this . . . we can always use a smart, hungry salesman," Mike said. "You stick around, do a bang-up job helping our reps place their orders, you can move up quick in this company."

Lopez nodded, adjusting his tie.

"I used to be in your spot," Mike continued. "Finishing college. Working an entry job here. Just work hard and you'll move up quick."

"You just might have to go out for beers with this guy someday," Lopez said, giving Mike a manly slap on the back.

Ernesto managed a smile. Mike reminded him of his father—the beer gut, the deep belly laugh. His father also used phrases like "bang-up job" when he spoke about work over dinner before he would pass out on the couch watching TV. In his teenage years Ernesto swore he would never grow up to be like his father: a man who gave most of his vitality to a job instead of his family.

Before the clock hands struck 5:00 p.m., Ernesto clocked out. With his crumpled paper bag in hand, he sped out of the cafeteria, past the cubicles, and waved good-bye to Jeanene as he zipped past the front desk and the toilet perched on top of the revolving pillar. Once he reached his rinky-dink Hyundai, Ernesto pulled out his cell phone. He planned to call his boss at Excel Staffing Solutions. "It's just not a good fit," Ernesto rehearsed to himself, using their language. But as he placed his thumb over the call button, he snapped the phone shut. He turned the ignition. He drove out of the parking lot. A few blocks away he sat in the midst of bumper-to-bumper traffic merging onto the highway. He hung his head over the steering wheel.

Gail sat on the couch when he stepped into her apartment. She was dressed in a tank top and yoga pants that showed her toned legs. The TV was turned to a cooking show.

"Hey babe," Gail said as he bent over to kiss her. "How was your second day?"

"It was okay," Ernesto said unconvincingly. He sat at the other end of the couch to untie his shoes. With a hangdog expression, Ernesto leaned forward with his elbows digging into his thighs. "I'm not sure if I'm going back tomorrow."

"What happened?"

Ernesto shook his head. "Nothing really. It just doesn't feel right. Everyone there is weird . . . at least the people who've been there for a while. I overheard these two guys talking about a Coke commercial like it was the most interesting thing. There's just something wrong with them."

The sound of someone chopping onions and peppers filled the silence between them.

"Today I met this guy who reminds me of my dad. Your typical good ole' company man. This place is good for people like him. People who *want* to be a company man."

"Soooooo, you're going to go back to your old security job? You're going back to a job you don't need a degree for?"

Ernesto threw his hands up. "I don't know. I don't know what I wanna do."

He ambled to the bathroom. He unbuttoned his shirt and peed. As he washed his hands, Gail stepped into the doorway.

"Have you checked in with the other staffing agencies?" she asked.

"Can you just drop it? For a minute, at least, please."

Gail rolled her eyes. She marched back to the living room.

"There go our plans to move out together because, you know what, I'm not paying for your rent," she shouted. "And you better not leave the toilet seat up again!"

"Come on, you don't have to say that. I'm still not sure if I'm leaving. And if I do, I'll find another job."

"Oh yeah, doing what?"

Ernesto sat on the couch. "I don't know. I could get a different office job at a place where they *don't* worship toilets. Or I can take some graphic design classes?"

"So more schooling?"

"Yeah."

"Oh, Ernesto. You don't know what you want to do. But at least you like going to school."

"What is *that* supposed to mean?"

"Nothing."

Frowning, he stood and walked over to the kitchen. She followed.

"Anywho, I'm sorry if I upset you," Gail said. She wrapped her arms around his waist. "How about you put on your uniform tonight, officer. I can be the new receptionist."

Ernesto tittered. "I wish you *were* our new receptionist. We could make the supply closet our private office."

They kissed. She ran her hand through his hair.

"Just go back tomorrow," Gail said. "You don't have to work there *forever*, silly. Just until you get some more experience on your résumé so you can move on."

He sighed and looked off.

"Come on. You know I'm right."

She pulled him in tighter.

"Okay, okay."

Later that night Ernesto could not fall asleep as he lay in Gail's bed. He had to wake up early the next morning to shave and iron his slacks and the new striped button-down shirt she had bought him. His thoughts a jumbled blur, he tossed and turned because he was afraid he would oversleep. Faint light trickled through her window's veiled curtains. He turned toward Gail and mistook the back of her head for Mrs. Banke's. This startled him. He leaned over her and squinted until his half-asleep mind confirmed he was indeed sleeping beside his girlfriend and not his butt-germ-hating workplace superior.

Ernesto turned back to his side. He stared at the curtains. Silhouetted by orange streetlight, he noticed, for the first time, that her bedroom window was barred.

WE ALL FALL

Raúl, a young, stocky Latino with a scraggly beard, sits behind the wheel of his parked car on bustling Clement Street just as a pregnant woman in her early thirties staggers and clutches the parking meter in front of him. His eyes widen as he watches her partner put his hand on her back and ask if she's all right. His grip on the steering wheel tightens as she shuts her eyes and exhales deeply. He then flings the car door open.

"Do you guys need some help?" Raúl asks.

"No, no, we're okay," the man says.

"You sure? I can drive you both to the hospital."

"I'm okay," she says, putting a hand out. "My water just broke. Believe me, it's a mess down there."

Raúl tries hard not to stare at the small puddle of water pooling between her shoes.

"All right, well, good luck. Hope you get to a hospital soon."

"That's the plan," the man says before he bounds down the sidewalk.

As he walks away, Raúl peers back at the woman. She bends forward, wrapping her arms around her bulging belly. Two elderly Asian women stand outside the local food market and stare at her. He takes two steps toward the pregnant woman, ready to run back to her aid, just as a Caucasian woman steps forward. She rubs the woman's arm and asks if she can help. *You're useless*, Raúl thinks to himself, trudging down the crowded sidewalk.

He remembers the time he accompanied his last girlfriend, Sofia, to a Planned Parenthood clinic. *Oprah* played from the television in the waiting area. He was the only guy there. He hid behind his book while he waited. He could still remember how gingerly Sofia walked back out into the lobby. All he could do was hold her hand and open the front door for her.

Raúl steps into a bakery near the corner of 3rd Avenue. As he takes his place in line, he remembers that there's a liquor store a block and a half away. It's on the way to his car. He could buy a fifth of rum, a bottle of Coke to chase it. It's Saturday; he has the rest of the day to himself. His roommates are out. It could be a one-time thing—the first time in six months he would drink some booze. After tomorrow—if there's any rum left—he'll simply pour it out in the sink, and that will be the end of that. A one-time deal. Not so bad. Besides, what are the odds of seeing a pregnant woman's water break in public? How often is he reminded that he should be the father of a three-year-old?

With a baguette tucked under his arm, Raúl marches down the sidewalk. He stares at the pavement. Once he approaches his car, he is careful to keep it in his periphery. He doesn't want to catch a glimpse of the liquor store on the corner.

Back behind the wheel, Raúl pulls out his wallet. Tucked behind his license is the business card of his AA sponsor, Jerry, a tenant lawyer who almost ruined his career with drinking. His number is already in Raúl's cell phone, but he wants to look at the note Jerry wrote on the back of the card. "We all fall," it read in neat handwriting. "It doesn't mean you're bad. Or weak. Don't ever forget that."

But then there was that thought again: it's only one time. *One time.* One time you *allow* yourself to fail. We all fall, at some point or another. It's inevitable.

Once home, Raúl sets a black plastic bag on the dining table. He places the baguette next to a fruit bowl. No one is home. *Hurry up*, he thinks to himself, opening a cabinet, snatching a drinking glass, and swinging the freezer door open to grab the ice-cube tray and twist two cubes out. They clink as they fall into the glass.

Raúl shuffles into his bedroom carrying the glass and the bag. His bedroom is suffused in sunlight. He sets the bag on his desk. He takes out the fifth of rum and liter of Coke. He stares at the bottle, at the rum's light-brown shade as sunlight glimmers on it. He can feel the burning sensation it would make in his throat if he took a slug from the bottle. *Stop*, he tells himself as he twists the cap off. He takes a deep breath then staggers to the lounge chair in the corner of his room. His photo albums rest on the bookshelf beside him. All he has to do is pivot and grab the album that contains pictures of his three years alongside Sofia. She was the only one who really knew him, the only one who accepted him for who he was—until she gave up on him just like all the others.

He stares at the bottle of rum then the pictures of his

parents resting on his desk. He put them through hell—
the drunk-driving accident; the bill for his three-week
stint in rehab; the time his mother had to leave work in
the morning to bail him out of jail after a highway cop
saw him pulled over on the shoulder, puking as he drank
and drove to work.

Sofia had been pregnant for two and a half months.
They drank and smoked almost every day during that
time. She didn't know she was pregnant, and how could
he? They were both twenty-three then. They weren't
ready to be good parents, though he heard, a year after
they split, that she was getting married to one of their
high school classmates. She had gotten herself cleaned
up, and they already had a kid.

Raúl buries his face in his hands and sobs, the bottle of
rum beside him.

INDOMESTICADO

When I walked up to my brother Eduardo's house for his daughter's birthday—salsa music booming for all the neighborhood to hear, kids bouncing in the inflatable pink castle on the lawn, los adultos standing in a line in the driveway for tacos—he hugged me and put his arm around my back like I should be proud of him.

"Here's my regalito para Lili," I said, handing him a gift bag.

"Gracias, hermano," Eduardo said. He was dressed in long khaki shorts, a blue Hawaiian shirt, and white sandals. His gold watch glimmered in the sunlight. "Grab some tacos. The caterers just started serving. Want a beer?"

"You got Pacífico?"

"I'll bring it out," Eduardo said with a wink before he beelined into his house. With his spiky hair and chin-strap beard he had the responsible-yet-hip-young-father act down. I used to want to be like him.

As I took my place at the end of the line, I scoped it out

for any good trim. But there was nothing—one ruca whose best days had long passed. Las viejas sitting at the picnic tables weren't any better. They all looked like they were married. Settled down. Madres instead of mamacitas. If they weren't feeding their babies they were eating like it was nothing but a necessity so they could keep an eye on their little demonios tearing around the yard. Meanwhile, the DJ played a classic cumbia that made me feel old and out of place—the single guy at a kids' party. I could've been home or at one of my shops working on my latest reclamation: a 1970 Plymouth Road Runner with Jamaica Blue paint. And to top it off, our mom, nuestro viejita—la gran criticona—was coming over. I had four-to-one odds that at some point she'd ask me something along the lines of "When are you going to settle down and give me a grandchild?"

I packed a girly-looking paper plate with food then took a seat at an empty table. Each one was decorated with a Tinkerbell table cover. I put my shades on like I didn't want anyone to recognize me. My brother and his wife, Tanya, made the rounds. They brought liters of soda and small pitchers of beer to the tables. First time I saw that at one of these fiestas. Usually it was only cans of Tecate, bottles of Corona. My big brother had Sierra Nevada on tap—fancy for us Latinos.

Eduardo nudged me when he dropped off my beer.

"Hermanito, check out that woman in the blue dress," he whispered, nodding at this curvy ruca at another table. "She's single. ¿Qué te parece?"

"She's all right, but she's got kids, right?"

"Un hijo, but that's it. She's a friend. I can set you both up," he said. He gave my bicep a squeeze.

"Ah, c'mon bro, you know that's not how I roll. And *believe me*, I got no trouble bringing the ladies back home. If anything, I've been spending too much time on my back."

I laughed. He shook his head and left. Though I wish he did, he could never understand why I played on so many ladies after my last relationship. Every once in a while he'd take up our viejita's company line and tell me, "Pick a good one, Tomás! And treat her right"—as if that's all there fucking is to it.

"Tío, come here!" Lili called from her castle. I put down my beer. I stepped over to a pile of kid shoes by the castle.

"Feliz cumpleaños, Lili," I said. She scurried over and hugged my leg. I bent over to put my arms around her. Mi sobrina was wearing a pink summer dress. She wore the Hello Kitty hairclip my ex, Pilar, had given her years ago.

"Did you bring me a present?" she said, staring up at me with her big brown eyes.

"I sure did. How old are you now?"

"Seven!"

"You're getting old, Lili. Pretty soon you won't be a princess. You'll be a queen!" I said, waving at Tanya.

"Nah uh. Mom's *always* gonna be the queen!"

Tanya gave me a hug hello, then she went from table to table asking the guests if they needed anything. She was a fine-ass woman. She wore a yellow blouse with a ruffled collar tied at her neckline, which was a damn shame because she had a nice rack, as if Diosito himself had personally sculpted her. Tanya waltzed about in tacónes, sporting some tight jeans that showed off her legs and curves. What made her different was that, unlike other foxy rucas, she didn't fall back on her good looks. She

106

didn't use her body to snatch up some high-rolling Silicon Valley gringo looking for an exotic trophy. She was smart, ambitious, down-to-earth, and took good care of her family. Ever since she became a part of la familia, mi viejita has gone on and on about how I need a woman like her. The funny thing is that *I tried* to be a good man—a man committed to one woman like our old man before he died when we were in high school. It's like mi viejita forgot about all those good girls I dated throughout my twenties, since none of them stuck. Pilar and I were together for three years. I had thought she was my lady and even had my sights on a ring, but I never got around to buying it since she quit on me, making up some bullshit excuse for what she did by saying we weren't as compatible as we should be.

I ate my flautas con arroz y frijoles at my table. A few more families I didn't know showed up. These kids' birthday parties always shake out the same way: the kids screaming and running around like they have Fanta for blood; at least one of the mothers shouting at them for being out of control; las mujeres tending to their babies while the men slink off to some corner to drink and bullshit until their old ladies tell them it's time to bounce. Liliana's fiesta was no different. Past the castle, los padres—at least those who showed up—were kicking it by the curb. They drank Coronas next to a pickup truck full of paint buckets and construction tools.

And that's when shit went down.

A big black truck with tinted windows rolled up to their driveway. The kids were buzzing around, jumping in and out of the castle or tearing around the yard playing hide-and-seek. That's when I saw Tanya freeze on the lawn as she saw the truck parked in front of their house. She glanced around real quick, probably to see if my brother was around. She looked like she'd seen a ghost. She marched over to the truck like she was *pissed*.

I couldn't see who she talked to though I was pretty damn sure it was some vato because women usually don't drive big-ass trucks like that. Tanya crossed her arms, her back all straight. It was no hi-and-how-are-you-this-fine-afternoon kind of discussion. She looked like she wanted that truck to get the fuck out of there, like she didn't want the men drinking by the street to overhear her. And then, just as quick as it came, the truck bailed, tires squealing, motor roaring, leaving behind the smell of burnt rubber just as my brother strolled out of the house holding a pitcher of beer. Like a few of the other adults, he watched the truck race down the street with a qué-chingados-was-that look on his face. Tanya strode past him. Flashing a big smile, she made her way to the nearest table where she asked one of her comadres, "You want some more soda?" like nothing had happened. I couldn't believe what I was seeing. I could feel my stomach knot. I knew something wasn't right with this picture.

The DJ faded the music down to announce the breaking of la piñata. And then my viejita showed up.

Once she greeted Eduardo and Tanya and handed Lili her present, I took off my shades and walked over.

"¿Cómo estas, ma?" I said, kissing her cheek. "You look nice." Mi viejita wore black linen pants and a white blouse with a floral design. It made her seem younger than the dark, formal clothes she usually wore.

"Estoy bien. ¿Y tu, mijo?"

"I'm all right."

Mi viejita took in the scene—the hired DJ, the taco caterers, all the families gathered and kids running around. She smiled as if there was magic fairy dust in the air. I looked around for Tanya.

"This is nice, huh?" she said as we sat down.

"Huh, yeah," I said, thinking, *Looks can deceive.*

"So how's work?"

"Todo bien."

She was quiet. I could tell she was working up to something.

"You need a house like this," she said. "You could sell one of your shops and keep the other one. Wouldn't that give you enough money to put a down payment for a house?"

"Dios mio, you're starting *already*?" I said.

"What do you mean starting already?"

"You're gonna lecture me *again* about buying a house, at your nieta's birthday party? And just what would I do with a big house all to myself? Ask our family if anyone wants to come up and try to make it in America? Or rent out the bedrooms to some paisanos and *all* their kids?"

Mi viejita crossed her arms. "You should be thinking of your future. That's all I'm saying."

"Oh right, a future with some *wonderful* wife like Tanya, right? Any one will do, huh?"

She rolled her eyes. I took a long, hard slug from my beer.

"I can never talk to you," she said. She headed toward the tacos.

I looked around for my brother. He was off somewhere. My mother stopped to chat with Tanya on the lawn for a second. Tanya drank a Corona, which was unlike her.

She usually drank when their fiestas were winding down. She was staring off like she was thinking hard about something. Then she caught me watching her. Her eyes darted away. She sauntered into the house. That's when I knew she'd been fooling around with whoever drove up to the house. I wasn't born yesterday. I could feel my head get hot. I clenched my fists.

Lili and her friends gathered by a wooden post my brother had put up for the piñata. The kids in the castle ran out to strap on their shoes. Tanya's brother used a stepladder to tie a rope around the hook. The kids all stared up at the piñata as he tied it to the rope—the singular focus in that moment of their lives.

Eduardo walked out of the house holding a stick covered in gift-wrapping paper. He handed it to Lili as the kids spread out to give her room. Without a blindfold, she hopped to whack the piñata while Tanya's brother pulled on the rope. She reared back and took two wild swings before Eduardo leapt in and wrapped his arms around her.

"No, no Lili. Don't do it like that," he said. "Swing back and *down*, with short swings, like I taught you."

She hung her head. She took a step back before she looked up at the piñata.

"Concentrate!" Eduardo said. Poor Lili. My brother couldn't just let her hit a piñata for fun. He had to make it into some fucking competitive drill. I looked over at Tanya. She was forcing a smile like this was all right with her.

Once Lili hit the piñata, the DJ and the parents—especially my mother—chanted, "¡Ya le diste uno!" When she hit it again, they shouted, "¡Ya le diste dos!" This went on for a minute before my brother told her to give some other kid a shot. And so it went, kid after kid, flailing and missing and hitting the piñata and everyone cheering on. Once an arm hung off the piñata, Eduardo took the stick from one of the boys so Lili could bust it open. With Tanya standing beside him, he snapped pictures of their daughter as she smacked a hunk off the piñata. The kids went bonkers, darting to the ground to snatch up the candies. Mi viejita commented on how adorable they were while I ignored her.

Tanya's brother came back out with another piñata—a sparkling one with girly tassels. Just like before, the boys and girls took turns whacking it. Tanya was smiling and shouting with each hit. Fucking phony. I stood and marched over to her.

"Great party!" I said with a big, big grin that made her uncomfortable. "But why aren't you asking *me* if I need anything?"

"Oh, uh . . . what, what did you—"

"Beer," I said, like a jab. She raced off into the house. I had wiped that smile off her face.

Once the piñata cracked, Eduardo let his son, little Daniel, bust it open. Daniel was four. A real cute kid. Miniature version of my brother. He looked so happy and proud when all the toys and candies poured out of the piñata. Just like before, all the kids dove in like little hungry piranhas.

"All right damas y caballeros, we're going to keep the music going," the DJ said as the kids scooped up the last candies. "Give a hand to our birthday girl, Liliana, who is going to perform a few songs for you!"

As a cumbia faded in, Lili stepped out from a corner of

the house followed by Tanya. My niece had changed into a fancy light-green dress like Tinkerbell's. My brother handed her a microphone then nudged her out onto the lawn in front of everyone. Poor Lili stood stiff, holding the mic by her side. Eduardo stood behind her with a Bluetooth clipped to his ear like he was ready to talk business with someone important.

"Come on mijita, dance like we've practiced," he said.

Lili began to shuffle from side to side before belting out the opening line of Rocío Dúrcal's "Cuando Te Vayas." All the women clapped. One of the men on the street whistled. Tanya filmed Lili's performance with her phone. Once my niece settled into her dance and singing routine, Eduardo uncrossed his arms. I could see why Tanya had on a few occasions at family gatherings joked at how picky and demanding my brother could be. This was nothing new to me. I grew up with him. I'd seen him get pissed off if he ironed a crease in his pants badly, if one of his perfectly combed hairs got messed up when we horsed around, or when our viejita served him an egg cooked over easy with a broken yolk.

Eduardo stepped over to Tanya. Swaying to the music, he clapped as he watched their daughter sing. He had no idea—no fucking idea—what had happened earlier. No idea that everything around him could unravel, just like that.

As much as I love mi sobrina, I couldn't take the *American Idol* shit. After she started her second song, I walked over to the homies hanging by the curb. I had to talk to them. See if they overheard anything between Tanya and the truck driver.

I brought my beer, said what's up to them. I asked for a

light. A short guy wearing a Che Guevara shirt offered me one. He opened his jacket, showed me a bottle of tequila, and asked if I wanted to hit it. "Sure," I said and thanked him. We shook hands and introduced ourselves. His name was Roberto. We bullshitted for a while. I asked the other guys how they knew my brother or Tanya.

Before we knew it, the party was dying down. The sun was beginning to set. A few of the guys left. That tequila bottle had long since been killed. Roberto and I were alone. That's when I asked him if he'd seen the black truck roll by earlier. He nodded then took a sharp drag from his cigarette.

"Did ya see the driver?" I asked. "My sister-in-law didn't look too happy."

Roberto stared at me. "I didn't, but my cousin did. Saw him when he drove up to the house. Parecía hispano."

"Did ya hear what they talked about? That's my brother's wife, bro."

"I know, primo. I know," Roberto said, exhaling a plume of smoke. "When she walked up to the truck, I heard her say 'What are you doing here?' He laughed. Her eyes looked like fire, mano. Then she said something like, 'I told you I can't keep doing this.' That's when he took off."

I took one last drag from my cigarette before I flicked it out on the street. That's when I knew she was just another fucking cheater.

I thanked Roberto, told him to stop by any of my shops if he ever needed some work done on his truck. Then I helped my brother clean up the front yard.

The sky was dark, nuestra viejita long since gone. Only Tanya's brother was around, helping to put away the fold-up tables. I couldn't bring myself to tell my brother.

Didn't want to shatter that castle of his. Eduardo never asked about the truck. Never asked if I saw what happened. He was still playing the part of the perfect dad of the perfect family.

The next day, early Sunday morning—when I was usually hungover or showing my fuck buddy the door—my phone was blowing up. It was Eduardo.

"What's going on, bro?" I said, still in bed.

He was crying. I hadn't seen him cry since his wedding day, eight years before.

"Tanya's been cheating on me," he said. "I can't be home with her right now. Can I come over?"

Twenty minutes later, he showed up at my condo with a six-pack of Pacífico left over from the party. His hair was all messed up like he hadn't showered, and he had bags under his eyes. Once I closed the front door, I hugged him hard. He sobbed. I didn't know what to do other than pat him hard on the back and tell him it's gonna be all right. Sunday mornings he was usually at church con su familia.

We sat on the couch. I popped open two beers. He needed to get loose. Let that shit out. As we drank Eduardo told me that their phone rang at one in the morning the night before. He startled up in bed because he thought it was bad news from our family in Jalisco.

"I said hello a couple of times, but they said nothing back," he said. "I could tell someone was on the line, listening to me, and then they hung up. Tanya was sitting up next to me. I turned the lamp on. I asked her who the man she talked to in the truck was. One of Tanya's comadres at the party told me about it, told me what she saw. Tanya's mouth was all open like when she's scared.

She just sat there and didn't say a thing. I *knew* that man in the truck was the one who had just called, so I asked her again, 'Who is he, Tanya?' And that's when she started crying."

I put my arm around him. "It's gonna be okay, hermanito," I said. "It's gonna be okay." And I knew it would be—someday. But who knows when.

We drank. He told me about the surprise getaway he was planning for their anniversary in two months. Mi pobre hermano.

Before we started on a third beer, Eduardo put his hands out and said, "Okay, I've got to get a hold of myself." It was like normal-adult Eduardo had snapped back into action. He blinked and looked around my living room like he was coming to after getting clocked. I sat in a chair in front of him, elbows on my legs, my hands folded. I patted his thigh. I hadn't shown so much affection to him in a long time.

"You all right?" I said.

Eduardo patted my hand. He gritted a smile. He sank into the couch, tilted his head back, and sighed. Then he looked at me with this softness in his eyes I hadn't seen since we were kids.

"Is this how you felt when you found out Pilar was cheating on you?"

I took a deep breath and nodded.

BALLAD OF
A SLOPSUCKER

The parking lot at Horatio's was packed for the ten-year reunion of San Leandro High's Class of '87 and Elvis Borboa—who had been voted Most Likely to Be on MTV his senior year—sat in his car near the back of the lot, sucking on a cigarette like nicotine was oxygen. An hour before, he had stood in front of his closet mirror wondering, *Should I stay or should I go?* He tried on shirt after shirt until he narrowed it down to two—a long-sleeve button-down shirt so it'd look like he had made something of himself, or a striped polo shirt that said I-don't-really-give-a-shit-about-appearances-but-I'll-look-presentable. No matter which one he wore, Elvis saw a twenty-eight-year-old straight-edge Latino reflected back to him—the cropped hair, fitted jeans, and a shirt that covered the flaming skull tattoo on his right shoulder. As he stared at himself, he couldn't help but wonder if the teenage, fuck-authority version of himself would have hated who he had become: just another tool; another sellout working for a big bank.

While he sat in his new Honda Accord, he couldn't shake the nervous, twisted feeling in his stomach. He popped the Eagles's *Greatest Hits* into the CD player. He skipped to "Best of My Love," which was totally un-metal of him. A long drag from his cigarette followed. It had been months since he had smoked. Oddly enough, the song soothed him even though it reminded him of Susana, his ex-girlfriend from high school. Ever since they graduated, he had occasionally daydreamed of playing and dedicating that song to her (which was *totally* un-metal of him).

After he flicked the cigarette out the window, Elvis flung the car door open. He strode across the parking lot. On his way to the entrance, he noticed a few faces that looked familiar. He couldn't remember their names, but he knew they were smart kids back in school. Would they recognize him now? Would *anyone* recognize him?

Standing by the entrance, next to the part of the restaurant that resembled a kitschy lighthouse, was Joey Marchment. He was smoking a cigarette by himself. Back in high school he was a quintessential stoner-skateboarder. He had gone to a couple of Elvis's shows. Shit, they even shared a joint at one of their high school parties. Joey had also cleaned himself up for the occasion. Dress shirt, pair of khakis, shiny dress shoes instead of his old Dr. Martens. His bleach-blonde hair—which used to be long and greasy as if he flipped burgers for a living—was now short, thinning, and slicked back. Like Elvis, he had developed a respectable beer paunch.

"Elvis Borboa?" Joey said.

"What's going on, Joey," Elvis said, shaking his hand. "Glad you remember me."

"Of course, man. You were Elvis, the heavy metal god!"

Elvis used to be the front man of a thrash metal band he started at San Leandro High with his best friend, Dontae. The band's name was Slopsucker. In high school Elvis sported long, curly black hair, torn-up jeans, and a black leather jacket his dad had handed down to him.

"You still play?" Joey asked.

"Nah, man." Elvis couldn't help but hang his head.

"That's too bad. I remember you used to *shred*."

"Yeah, well, you know, it's one of those things. Hardly anyone can pay the bills playing a six-string."

"Fucking A, man, fucking A," Joey said, nodding and slowly turning his head like he was watching a thought gently bob away.

Inside, Elvis heard a loud hum of chatter around the corner. *Goddamn it*, he thought. People were already asking about his former musical self.

A sign by the front podium read, "Class of '87 Reunion!" An overly smiley Asian woman with a name tag that read "Annie Chow" sat behind a long table covered with rows of printed name tags. They exchanged pleasantries. Elvis remembered she was a major kiss-up in school. She parked her rear front row and center in their physics class so she could laugh at all the inane jokes from their teacher along with all the other voracious grade-grubbers. On top of being pretty, she had always been smart and driven. Once he saw the big glittery rock on her ring finger, Elvis figured she got just about everything she ever wanted in life.

He saw his name tag on the table. He scanned the remaining ones for Susana and Dontae's. They were MIA. Were they coming? Were they already there? Would they talk to him, or tell him to fuck off? Would Susana be there with someone? A boyfriend? Husband? What if she was inexplicably free after all these years?

The classy restaurant overlooked the San Leandro Marina. The dining area around the bar was roped off for their reunion. All the tables had been cleared out so everyone could mingle. Seventy or eighty people convened throughout the room. Most of his old classmates had dressed up as if they were dining at a posh restaurant in San Francisco, the city he had called home since graduating from high school. Booming laughter from the patio startled him. There was so much happening around him. Before he realized what he was doing, Elvis beelined to the bar. He could've walked past Gandhi, Cindy Crawford, or Ozzy Osbourne and not noticed them. Man, did he need a drink.

As he leaned against the counter, staring at the bartender, trying to will him to look his way, Elvis scanned the bar as though his birth name was Cool Breeze. He locked eyes with a classmate whose name tag read "Mindy Roberts." Her jaw dropped. She waved with such glee that he waved back, although he had never—as far as he remembered—had a conversation with her. Two stools down from Mindy was George, a wild-haired Samoan who had streaked across the football field during a homecoming game Susana had dragged him to. And then there she was: Susana. The woman of his sad and sorrowed dreams of unrequited love. She stood in a circle of women gathered at the other end of the bar. His heart bottomed. She was fucking gorgeous and cute as ever—the same big brown eyes, light-brown skin, and magnetic smile that drew people to her. Her black hair fell over the straps of her blue summer dress. Elvis thought she had never looked so beautiful—except maybe at the junior prom they had gone to together.

Once he spotted her, Elvis was done for; he couldn't keep himself from stealing glances at her. After all those years they were actually in the same room. And to his complete and dizzying surprise she seemed to be alone. No possible significant other satellited around her.

While he watched her, Elvis couldn't help but remember—as much as he didn't want to—the last time they were together.

🍾

It all went down on a Saturday afternoon, less than two months before their senior prom. Elvis was in his bedroom restringing his black Jackson King V guitar. Venom's classic *Black Metal* blared from his stereo. It was 1987, a year after thrash metal's zenith when Metallica's *Master of Puppets*, Slayer's *Reign of Blood*, Megadeth's *Peace Sells . . . but Who's Buying?*, and Kreator's *Pleasure to Kill* came out. Elvis's dad was in the backyard, working in his shed, when his mom knocked on the door.

"Yeah," Elvis shouted over the music.

"Susy's here for you!" she yelled from behind the door where Elvis had taped a poster of Machu Picchu shrouded in mist. "Shit," he said to himself. He took a deep breath as he lurched to the front door.

Susy stood on the other side of the screen door. She wore a black tank top, faded blue jeans, and the green Chuck Taylors he had doodled on with a permanent marker. (He had scribbled "Elvis lives!" on the back heel.) She was concealing something behind her back.

"Hey, you wanna come in?" Elvis said, creaking the screen door open.

"That's okay," Susy said. "My dad's taking us out to lunch with one of his friends. I was running some errands and just wanted to pop in to give you a surprise."

"Oh yeah, what you got?"

Though he was trying to play it cool, Elvis could feel his stomach knot. The night before, he had snuck out to hit up a party without Susana. Celeste White, the lead cheerleader at San Leandro High, had invited him. Celeste White, the hottest girl in school, had flirted with him. She professed to Elvis that she liked him. This was certifiable wet dream material. To boot, she kept putting her hand on his arm and brushing her blonde hair while they talked. After he stumbled back home in a fog of blissful drunken stupor, he woke up thinking about how good it would have felt to make out with her. To have his hands all over her. The only reason he kept his paws to himself was because he and Susy had been together for two years.

Susy handed him a mixed tape. On the cassette case spine she wrote "Heavy Shit" and drew a smiley face. Years later, remembering those details slayed him.

"I really liked your last mix," she said. "I think you're right . . . the Scorpions *are* the best thing to ever come out of Germany."

Elvis combed his long hair to the side so it wouldn't cover half of his face. He stared off at the front lawn. Earlier that morning he had convinced himself to break up with her. He just didn't know when to pull the plug.

"You okay?" she asked. Elvis had not hugged and kissed her like he typically would when she'd come over.

121

"Yeah, I'm just tired. Wait . . . let me walk you to your car."

Susy marched to her old gray car parked in front of his parents' house. He followed. She walked with her head lowered, staring at the walkway like she knew something was up. Afterward, Elvis wondered if she could sense what was coming.

"Your mind seems to be somewhere else," Susy said as they approached her car.

Elvis took a breath. "Susy, this is something I've been thinking about for some time. I'm just, uh . . . I, umm . . . I think we should date other people."

Elvis never forgot the face Susy made—her mouth dropping, her eyes opening wide.

"Are you *serious*?" she said, staring up at him. She took a step forward. "You've been *thinking about this* for some time? Since when?"

"I don't know. It's been a while."

"So why are you saying this to me now? You wanna go out with someone else? Is that it?"

Elvis took a step back. He thought she might try to slap him.

"Who is it, Elvis? Who is it?"

"It's no one, Susy! I'm just afraid of this getting too serious. I'm sorry. I don't know how else to say it."

"So what are you *really* saying? Are you breaking up with me? Is that what you're trying to tell me?"

"No, Susy. I just . . . think it'd be a good idea if we saw other people."

Susy crossed her arms. She glared at him until he looked away. "That's bullshit. And I am *not* okay with us seeing other people. If all you want to do is break up with me, then grow some damn balls and do it."

Susy brushed past Elvis and stormed to the driver's-side door. Once she fumbled for her keys, she stomped back to him.

"Give it to me," she said.

She snatched the tape from Elvis, threw it on the sidewalk, and smashed the case with her foot. She flung the door open and slammed it before she drove off with the motor roaring.

Broken cassette in hand with its tape dangling, Elvis walked back into his house. He bunched up the loose tape in his hand. He didn't want his mom to see it and ask what had happened.

In his room, the door closed, Elvis flipped through his milk crate full of albums. He took out Metallica's *Ride the Lightning*. The album cover had an electric chair floating in a dark sky with bolts of lightning. He cued the record to "Fade to Black." He blasted it, all dramatic, then he lay on his bed, hands cupped behind his head, clutching the cassette as the opening guitar notes filled the room. He stared at the picture of his idol, Tom Araya—the Chilean bassist and lead singer for Slayer— taped on the ceiling above his bed. He felt shitty about what he'd done. They had been friends since junior high when he and Susy took Spanish classes together (the equivalent of Rob Halford taking beginner's classes for heavy metal screeching). During sophomore year he walked her home practically every day unless she was working on the school paper, having soccer practice, or attending one of her Chicano-power MECHA meetings. Susy had lost her virginity to him. That was a big deal to him as well. And she was the first girl—and maybe the only one—he had ever loved.

By then Elvis was getting caught up in all his self-hype about their band, especially after Slopsucker blew away the other musical acts at their school talent show. He truly believed that part of his life was merely the beginning of something bigger. His bandmates, Dontae and White Trash Phil, talked about becoming the best thing to come out of shit town San Leandro, like how Metallica's Cliff Burton had come out of neighboring Castro Valley to become the most badass metal bassist on the planet. Elvis didn't want to be like everyone else. He didn't want to turn out like his mom and dad, who never seemed happy—more like they were stuck with one another. He wanted a rock 'n' roll kind of life: the thrill he'd get when he would thrash his head and flail on a guitar. The way he felt ten feet tall onstage in front of a crowd. The communion he felt playing with his bandmates. "It's one life you live," his father—a former bohemian—liked to tell him. Una vida. Susy was a way cool chick, but Celeste White—the girl *every* straight guy in the locker room openly fantasized about—was the Big Leagues. Susy didn't fit in with the flashy, VH1 behind-the-scenes documentary Elvis thought his life could become. He was afraid that he and Susy would turn out like his mom and pop someday. He was afraid of growing up to become like his dad, living his dreams vicariously through one of his children since he was too chickenshit to have truly chased them when he was younger.

After "Fade to Black" ended, the turntable needle hissed on a constant loop. Elvis leapt off his bed. *Fuck it*, he thought, chucking the tape into his trash can. In that moment he practically thought of their breakup as some life lesson; he rightly figured life would have its share of difficult decisions he would have to make. Like dumping a sweet girl for the hottest chick in school.

Ten years later, Elvis regretted their breakup more than anything in his life.

🍾

Susy continued to chat with her old high school friends at the end of the bar. A pool of sunlight fell upon them. As Elvis stared at Susy, he fleetingly remembered—the self-suffering masochist he was—the first time they drove up to the San Leandro Hills to watch a sunset together. A bartender came over and snapped him back into the present. Elvis needed a tonic of liquid courage. And so he ordered his old standby: a beer and a cheap shot of whiskey. He downed it and walked over to Susy.

Elvis stood on the periphery of her circle. He looked off, pretending to be enraptured with the action around the bar while sneaking glances at Susy. He did this for what seemed like the most eternal minute of his life before she noticed him. Elvis grinned at her, all hopeful. Susy stared back at him with a blank expression before she forced a grin. He squirmed from the awkwardness. He didn't know what to do—try to interject in their conversation, or quietly walk away without anyone noticing him. Before long a classmate put her hand on Susy's shoulder. Her face lit up when she turned and recognized her friend.

Beer bottle in hand, Elvis retreated to the snack table next to the windows. He said hello to a short Filipino who had been standing there. It dawned on Elvis that he had stumbled upon the corner of the restaurant where single men hid in an attempt to gather themselves. It was reunion Limbo. His shoulders felt tight. Staring out at the twinkling marina, he gobbled some crab cakes and inhaled some fried calamari. Then he noticed the back doors. Now was his chance. He could just leave. He would never see any of these people again. It was a mistake to have come.

Just then, a collective roar of laughter emerged from the restaurant patio. Like a few others standing around him, Elvis turned to see what all the hoopla was about. He saw Dontae, clapping his hands and laughing with his characteristic abandon as he stood tall among the group surrounding him.

Arm in arm with brown bags in hand, Elvis and Dontae staggered into the crowded kitchen of a party in the Mission District. It was 1991. That night, Slopsucker opened for Death Angel at the Kabuki. They played in front of hundreds of metalheads who filled the theater and its balcony. After the show the band sold most of their LPs and all of their shirts, which had a drawing of a crayfish bent over puking on another crayfish that had passed out face first in a pool of vomit. It was Slopsucker's biggest gig to date—and ultimately would be their biggest ever. A week before, they had wrapped up their second West Coast tour, rolling through Chico, Reno, Portland, Olympia, Seattle, and Boise in the clunky white van they dubbed "Old Bertha." The boys never forgot that Boise gig; their set abruptly ended after the third song because two redneck hicks kept staring at Dontae while making gorilla-grunting sounds between songs. After Elvis, White Trash Phil, and Dontae leapt off the stage to confront these future gas station attendants, their club security had to keep the bandmates at bay. Beer bottles were flung. Yelling ensued. The band managed to escape by sneaking their gear out of the back of the club.

Like ravenous pirates staring upon their hard-earned loot, Elvis and Dontae came upon the kitchen counter, teeming with half-empty bottles of booze. Although Elvis was five foot ten—tall for a full-blooded Peruvian—Dontae dwarfed him; he had a taut build with a mini-fro that made him seem even taller. He wore a black Misfits shirt with ripped jeans while Elvis donned a Slayer shirt he had cut into a tank top. Their shirts were still damp with sweat from their gig. As Elvis snatched a bottle of whisky, two metalheads decked out in denim and spikes slapped them on the back.

"Great fucking show, man!" they said, lifting their beer cans up to salute them.

"Right on, guys," Dontae said in his suave, cool voice before the two chums clanged the King Cobras within their brown bags with their fans' beer cans.

Throughout the night a parade of headbangers—including two cute, trashy girls Elvis and Dontae had never spotted at any of the local shows—congratulated them. One of the young ladies, a flaxen-haired damsel with green eyes that reminded Elvis of a cat, offered the bandmates homemade moonshine. And, well, they couldn't say no to that, so they took slugs from her flask. Dontae offered her a drink from his King Cobra. The two chums laughed their asses off when she proceeded to drain his entire forty. But even in that drunk-exalted moment, Elvis couldn't forget his mistakes from the past, because this reminded him of Susy—she had once shotgunned an entire can of beer.

Before long White Trash Phil joined their debauched revelry. He was a stout, thick-necked man with a bullring pierced through his nose. The three bandmates traded shots of whiskey and held court over the party, which was a mix of metalheads and hardcore punks they regularly saw at venues like Ruthie's Inn, the Fab Mab, or the Kabuki.

Late into the night, after too many drinks and a few bumps of coke in the bathroom, the attractive punk-rock girl approached them again with her pixie-haired friend. Elvis and Dontae smoked a joint on the back steps that looked out over a dark alley lined with cardboard boxes used for makeshift homes. By then Phil had already left with his Catch of the Night.

"So how did you two meet?" she slurred as Dontae handed her friend the joint.

"I met this motherfucker in junior high," Elvis said, putting his arm around Dontae, his voice raspy from screaming and growling at their show. "He was the first black dude I met who liked rock 'n' roll. Before I met him I didn't even know that was fucking possible! Thought y'all listened to nothing but the blues and hip-hop and ooh-uh-ooooooh, baby, baby!"

In a musical genre dominated by white bands and white fans, Elvis and Dontae were a rare breed. The black sheep among black sheep. In high school they used to hit up Tower Records and other music stores in the East Bay. They were almost always the only brown folks cruising the metal and punk aisles. Years later, once they attended punk and thrash metal shows in San Francisco and Berkeley, it was the same deal: they were usually the only POCs in attendance. Together they weathered the pits, always watching each other's backs. By the end of the night, pummeled and sweaty—sometimes bloodied—they would stand by the bar and drink to numb their adrenaline. Night after night the two went to war together and returned home with their ears ringing but their hearts full from the savagely beautiful music that coursed through their veins.

In the early morning dark, Elvis and Dontae stumbled back to their apartment with the two young ladies. For Elvis, she ended up being another in a medley of one-night stands. Dontae ended up dating his lady for a while. A few weeks later, on a night of partying at Elvis and Dontae's pad, she snapped a Polaroid of the two passed out on their ratty couch, their heads slumped together. Elvis put the photo up on their fridge along with flyers advertising their past shows. Since neither of the two had brothers, they would joke—usually when they were wasted—about how they were brothers from different mothers. Ever since they began jamming together during their freshman year at San Leandro High, Elvis could not imagine playing without Dontae.

But that's exactly what happened.

Months after they opened for Death Angel, after Slopsucker played another show in the city to about thirty folks—many of them their hard-partying friends—White Trash Phil quit the band. He told Elvis and Dontae that he was tired of playing the same gigs to the same people. The band was gearing up to record their second LP with songs like "Stinking Flesh," "Defile," and a raunchy number called "Wild Fur." Musically, the band had evolved; they were playing faster, playing longer songs with more elaborate chord changes, even playing in different time signatures, but that meant shit to Phil. "We can't just party forever," he told his younger bandmates. Elvis said he just no longer believed. Fuck him.

He and Dontae tried out a number of bassists, but none of them panned out. A few months later Dontae bowed out of the band. They had an epic spat at their pad, one Elvis could not recall since he drank like he was aiming for oblivion and subsequently blacked the fuck out. The next day he heard that he had smashed his Ibanez guitar against their fridge and all the pictures and concert flyers they had put up. One of their neighbors had called the cops on them, but Elvis only vaguely remembered that. A few days later Dontae moved out of the apartment they had shared in Hayes Valley for nearly three years. Elvis was twenty-two. Slopsucker had lasted six years. His Ibanez sat in a corner of the living room with a broken neck until Elvis crammed it into their trash can.

As one could expect, Dontae and Elvis drifted apart. The last he heard about Dontae was that he had moved down to LA. For a while Elvis was often the only brown skin moshing in the pits at local thrash shows until he gave that up too. Without his metal brother, it just wasn't the same.

Before Elvis stepped out to the patio, Dontae spotted him.

"Look at you," Dontae said, his head turned exaggeratedly to the side. "I almost didn't recognize you without all your hair."

"I almost didn't recognize *you* without all your hair," Elvis said, feeling a ridiculously huge grin dawn over him. Elvis put his arms around Dontae. They patted one another hard on the back.

"Still the same guy," Dontae said. He stepped back to size up Elvis. "Except . . . are you . . . getting pregnant?"

"Dude, shut the fuck up."

Elvis was overcome with a joy he had not felt in a long-ass time. He even waved and said hello to all their classmates standing around them. Dontae introduced Elvis to his girlfriend, Melanie, a bookish-looking black woman with an afro and cat-eye glasses.

"Dontae talked a lot about you on the drive up," Melanie said. "You used to be in the same band, right?"

"Yeah, we had a band called Slopsucker. Has Dontae played any of our LPs for you? We're probably the only two people in the world who still own them."

"That's not true. I bought one," a guy standing in their circle with a name tag that read "Billy" said. "I went to one of your shows in Berkeley."

"Right on, man," Dontae said, giving him a high five.

"Whatever happened to your band?" said a short woman with a squeaky voice.

Elvis peered over at Dontae. His eyebrows cocked, Dontae nodded to Elvis like he was saying, *You go right ahead.*

"We just . . . ran our course," Elvis said. "Happens all the time."

"Hey man, you wanna grab a drink?" Dontae asked,

putting a hand on Elvis's shoulder. "I need to refuel. Baby, you want anything?"

"I'm good. You two go ahead," Melanie said.

They put their arms around one another like old times.

"It's good to see you, man," Elvis said. "I was afraid you wouldn't come up."

"Word. Shit, I didn't know if you wanted to see me."

"Bro, that was a long time ago. If anything, I thought *you'd* be the one who wouldn't want to see me after the way I handled shit."

Dontae patted Elvis on his shoulder. "Its bygones, brother. I know it hurt. We broke up, you know."

Elvis grimaced. It was true. He glanced off in Susy's direction across the bar. After all those years it's like that wound was reopened. Elvis could still vividly remember the day after Dontae moved out. He remembered walking through their apartment to a near-empty living room. Dontae's absence felt heavy. The ratty couch they hauled in from a Goodwill. All his books. Records. Cassettes. Posters. His drum kit and bongos. Gone.

"Whatever happened to you after I left?" Dontae asked. His eyes had this softness that killed Elvis.

"I stayed at our old pad for another year. Got this Korean art-school girl to rent out your old room until we became more than just roommates. And of course that didn't end well, so I moved out. Now I got a studio apartment up in North Beach. It has a great fucking view of the city."

"I bet it does! That's cool, man. But what about your music? I could've sworn I heard you joined Angel Rot. I went to one of their shows, but you weren't with them."

Elvis told Dontae he briefly played for them after

Slopsucker went belly-up. What could he do: he was still addicted to the rush from being onstage, from seeing kids going bat shit berserk to their brutal music, but he was relegated to rhythm guitar and backing vocals. He also had zero songwriting input. In other words he went from being the main man to a regular chump. That fall was too much for him. And so—especially after he continued to get promoted at the bank he worked for—Elvis never made much time to play. He hung his head after he told Dontae all this.

"And what did you do with your drums?" Elvis asked.

"I still have them. It's a smaller kit now. Last year I started playing again. I jam with this jazz quartet that plays some Afrobeat."

"That's cool."

The bartender approached.

"You wanna get a shot for old time's sake?" Elvis asked.

Dontae looked at the bartender, then turned to Elvis with an awkward grin. "That's trouble, man. I'll pass. I don't drink like I used to, but I'll get this round."

Though his enthusiasm was deflated, Elvis ordered a shot of Cazadores while Dontae got a pint to share with his lady. The two former best friends clinked their glasses before Elvis downed his shot. Dontae began to amble back to the patio but stopped to wait for Elvis.

"You go ahead," Elvis said. "I'll see you out there."

Elvis watched Dontae walk back to Melanie. He turned back to the counter and eyed an empty stool at the end of the bustling bar. He pushed through the crowd before he slinked into it. There he was, like a broken record, by himself at another bar. His mouth all squiggly, Elvis lifted his hand to flag down the bartender. He wanted another shot, and then another one, and then another. He wanted to blur that emptiness he felt after talking to Dontae.

As he waited and waited for the bartender, getting more pissed off by the second, Elvis saw not only Susy but also Celeste White at the other end of the restaurant.

If he wasn't an atheist, Elvis would have sworn that the gods were conspiring against him. Making a cruel example of him.

He snickered to himself.

By the time he was twenty-five, Elvis had vowed to stop dating white women. The last one he dated, a gorgeous young woman from his office, told him to stress his Peruvian ancestry to her rich parents from Orinda since her daddy didn't like Mexicans. But dating Latinas from San Francisco didn't fare much better for him either. If they were smart and pretty they were too high-maintenance for his taste. And if they had personality they were usually too clingy, or too much drama. To make matters worse he couldn't find any Latinas who were into rock, none who were punk rock at heart like Susy. One young woman he dated told him she liked rock 'n' roll, but that meant Bon Jovi and Def Leppard, which he found appalling.

And so, the poor, lovelorn bastard couldn't help but think about Susy because that's what poor, lovelorn bastards do.

He mailed a letter to her folks' home. It was one of those hey-how-are-you-how-has-life-turned-out-for-you-I've-been-thinking-about-you kind of letters. To his surprise,

Susy wrote back. The letter was postmarked from Sunny-vale. She told him she'd heard of Slopsucker's "mild fame" since they had played a gig in downtown San Jose years before. She also informed him she had a boyfriend whom she met in college. Elvis was no fool. He got the hint.

Elvis fixated on one summer afternoon they had between their junior and senior years. He was driving his green Datsun (which he called "Booger" because of its color) down San Leandro Boulevard, beneath the BART train tracks. Susy was rocking her big sunglasses and a Clash T-shirt from their Combat Rock tour. Crammed in the back seat was his Marshall amplifier, a half stack of speakers, and his beloved Jackson guitar. He had picked Susy up from her home after band practice to hit up their favorite taquería on East 14th Street. The Scorpions's "No One Like You" began to play from the radio as they rolled up to a stoplight.

"This is my SONG!" Elvis said. He cranked up the vol-ume until the front speakers began to crackle. He whipped his head to the beat, windmilling his long, curly hair. "Just tell me when it's green. And take the wheel. I'll give the gas."

"You serious?" Susy said, chuckling mischievously.

He stopped headbanging and peered at her. "Yeah, I'm serious."

"Okay, just checking."

And then a Pontiac Firebird rolled up next to them.

"It's on, buddy, it's on!" Elvis said to the driver, con-tinuing to headbang while the song approached its epic chorus. The light turned. As Klaus Meine sung the cho-rus, Elvis made a guttural roar and floored the pedal as Susy squealed and grabbed the wheel, rubber peeling as his dingy car jetted across the intersection. They zoomed past the Firebird and rode down the street. Elvis and Susy laughed for a long time afterward. Anything seemed possible.

At the taquería Susy placed her order in perfect Spanish. She chatted up the woman behind the register like she was a friend of the family. Elvis and Susy sat down at a sun-filled table by a window. She drank from her horchata; Susy equated the drink to a magical tonic because drinking them always made her happy. Meanwhile he dipped a chip into a bowl of pico de gallo while keeping an eye on his car. Elvis felt proud to have watched her converse with the cashier. He felt proud to have a girlfriend who could show such genuine, non-bullshit warmth to strangers. He felt proud to have a girlfriend who was smart and driven but wild enough to hold the steering wheel while he headbanged and drove.

On the drive home they held hands over the parking break. Elvis told her he loved her when he parked in front of her parents' home. He could still faintly remember the smile on her face when she waved good-bye from the walkway.

Things between them seemed so easy. At least that's how Elvis remembered it. And it was never like that with any of the other women he would eventually date. Back then he had no idea how difficult it would be to find someone like Susy.

As the bartender attended to everyone piled in the middle of the bar, Elvis peered in Susy's direction. Their eyes locked for a few seconds. She had acknowledged him. Instead of ordering another shot, he asked for a glass of water. He downed a big gulp and wiped his lips.

Susy and her friends turned to Elvis once he stood before them.

"Hey there," Elvis said to them. "Hi, Susana."

"Hey Elvis," she said with a polite grin.

He took a step forward as though he was swooping in for a hug. And not just any run-of-the-mill hug; this was a validating, all-is-forgiven, Elvis, you're-not-a-stupid-prick hug. But Susy wasn't having it. She stood her ground. Elvis caught himself and put his hand out to try to cover up his misstep. Clutching his glass of water, he stepped back. His head drunkenly swayed. He looked at her, breathing her in after all those years. "You look gorgeous."

Susy furrowed her eyebrows. Her friends got all quiet.

"Uh, thanks, Elvis."

He tried to grin through the awkward silence.

"So . . . what have you been up to?" Susy asked, clasping her cocktail in front of her as though she expected him to entertain her. Elvis noticed the wedding band on her ring finger. And there went that pipe dream.

He cleared his throat. "I wouldn't know where to start!" he said, all their eyes on him. "It's been a really long time since we've seen each other."

"It has. I almost didn't recognize you without all your hair."

"I've been getting that a lot today." Elvis scratched the side of his head. Goddamn. God*damn* it. *You fucking idiot*, he thought. He was foolish to have come to this reunion thinking he might still have a shot at Susy. So fucking stupid.

"Well, I just wanted to drop by and say hi and tell you how nice it is to see you after all these years," Elvis said.

"Hey, it was nice to see you too," she said. "I'm glad you made it out."

Elvis raised his hand good-bye and turned away. He retreated, wandered off then spotted the patio area and remembered Dontae was out there. But he was in no mood to talk to him. Or anyone. And he was far from being in a festive mood, or pretending to be in one.

Before he turned to the patio, Elvis saw the back door that led out of the restaurant. He barged through it. The marina opened before him. Rows of docked sailboats gently rocked on the bay. Off in the distance the sun began to set over the hills in the Peninsula. A sidewalk winded along the shoreline. There was no one around, only a middle-aged couple strolling along the path. Elvis walked toward a bench overlooking the marina. He took a seat. Elbows on his knees, he bent forward and buried his face in his hands. He took a deep breath and sat there for a long time, covering his face. Then he heard foot-steps crunching over gravel, but he didn't sit up to make it appear as though he was simply taking in the view. He could not give a shit if someone from the reunion saw him like that. He would never see them again.

"Hey, man, you all right?" he heard Dontae say. Elvis looked up. "I saw you walk out of the restaurant."

"I'm all right." Elvis slid toward the side of the bench. "You don't happen to have any smokes, do you?"

"Your lucky day. That's *one* bad thing I still happen to do."

Dontae sat beside him. He held out a pack of Camels. He lit Elvis's cigarette then he lit one for himself.

"What's going on with you, bro? Even after all these years I can still tell when you're not doing good."

"Oh yeah? And what gave it away?"

Dontae nearly choked as he took a drag.

Elvis exhaled. "You remember how I used to be hung up on Susy?"

"Shit, bro. Don't tell me you still are."

"Come on, dude. You know me. I've always been a fucking idiot. Of course I'm still hung up on her. Do you know how many women I've gone out with, trying to find someone like her? I met the sweetest, most amazing girl of my life *when we were teenagers* . . . and I let her go. I let her go like she was an old guitar I didn't want."

They stared past the sailboats.

"This has just been too much, man. Seeing Susy, more beautiful than I ever remembered her, but she's married now. And having everyone remember me for being in a rock band. You know my old guitars, the Jackson I used to sleep with because I wanted it to feel like it was a part of me? And all my distortion pedals that we drove around everywhere looking for? I put them in my parents' garage. I fucking banished them from my life. I can't even look at them." Elvis hung his head. "This just isn't where I expected to be," he said, tears filling his eyes.

Dontae stared at his shoes. They sat in silence.

"But you seem happy, and I'm really genuinely happy about that," Elvis said. "I'm glad I got to see you and meet your lady."

Dontae put an arm around him. "You gotta get your head up again," he said. "Shit changes—snap—like that. We never know when things will turn, but what I *do* know is that you chased your dream, that you and I had the balls to even try. We got to play in front of hundreds of people. You wrote songs and lyrics that people *memorized.* We hit the road, holed up in the shittiest motels, and we played up and down the coast. We used to dream about doing that when we were kids. We fucking worked for it. We *made* that happen. *You* made that happen. All them people back there remember us for being in a band because a lot of them probably wished they could've done something like that at least once in their lives."

Elvis nodded. He couldn't deny it.

"Dude, don't you realize how many of our classmates never even got out of San Leandro? How many of them just started cranking out kids as soon as we were done with high school? I've heard it all night."

Elvis turned to Dontae. He leaned over and embraced him.

"You were always my bro," Elvis said, pounding his back. "I know this is going to sound sad, but our high school years were the happiest of my life."

"They were great times, but life isn't over. Come on, fucker. Let's go back in. I came here to see you. Don't let this shit end like this."

Elvis and Dontae and Melanie hung out on the patio the rest of the night. To his surprise Elvis enjoyed rekindling their high school days with their other classmates. They recalled the talent show during their senior year. The raging house party that was busted by the cops, which inspired a few of them to drunkenly jump a fence in an attempt to escape. And Elvis enjoyed hearing some of their surprising post–high school exploits, like a classmate who took a cruise to Antarctica. Or another classmate who got into rock climbing.

Toward the end of the evening, Susy and a few of their old punk rocker friends joined them. Once half of their class had left, Elvis and Susy chatted about her travels, her work in community engagement, and her parents. She asked about Elvis's family, his music, and what happened to Slopsucker. It was sad to rehash the band's history, but it wasn't as bad as when he first talked about it with Dontae. Conversing with Susy was a strange experience for him, especially after he had immortalized their time together for so many years. He even brought up the big looming but silent elephant in the room: her husband.

"So who's the lucky guy?" Elvis said, nodding at her wedding ring. "And why didn't you bring him along?"

"His name's Eduardo. He's the one I met in college. I wanted to bring him out, but then I figured it'd be more difficult to really catch up with all our old classmates. We figured he'd feel left out of a lot of conversations."

"Well, he's a really lucky guy. But I'm sure he already knows that."

Susy reared back ever so slightly and made a you-better-not-try-anything face.

"You were always amazing, Susy," Elvis said. "I was young, and I had no idea *how* special you were back then. I know that doesn't change anything now, but I had to get that off my chest."

"Well, you were always special to me too, Elvis," Susy said. "You were always a sweet guy beneath all that hair and leather. You never fooled me."

He blushed.

"Oh wait, did I tell you I still play?" Susy said.

"What, guitar?"

"Yeah! I have an acoustic. I'm sure my playing drives

Eduardo up the wall, but I still think I could end up being the spiritual love child of Nancy Wilson and Linda Ronstadt. And I owe it all to you and your tutelage."

Elvis wiped away an imaginary tear. Dontae had been standing to the side. He leaned in.

"You ever try playing an acoustic?" he asked Elvis.

"Not that I remember."

"You should give it a try. I know you, man, and I think there's still a voice inside you that wants to come out. But maybe all your old shredding gear isn't what it sounds like anymore."

Elvis furrowed his brow as though he had just been told his mother was the Queen of England.

"Take me as an example," Dontae continued. "You remember my double-bass pedals, right? Well, I don't play them anymore because it's just not me. I changed. I evolved."

"Dontae, you need to stop. I can't stand such blasphemy!"

A week later, Elvis took the 38 bus from work up to South Van Ness and Geary. He walked over to the new, huge Guitar Center a few blocks up. All that newfound magic was there again, like when his dad took him to a music shop for the first time when he was ten and he stared at all the guitars hanging on the walls like they were a galaxy of sound and possibilities. In their acoustic room, Elvis sat on a stool. He had the room to himself. He picked up a couple of guitars and strummed a few chords. Their sound reverberated through the room. In that moment, that was his world—just him and that guitar and the sound they created together. He strummed one whose resonant tone sounded like the one he heard in his head when he thought of what an acoustic should sound like. He curled over its body. He closed his eyes and put his ear to it as he plucked the lower E string. It felt right—the way it sounded. The way it fit in his arms.

That night, for the first time in years, Elvis strode down the city streets with a guitar bag strapped to his back. He was surprised how familiar it still felt, as though he had never stopped. His long, black hair and torn jeans, nicked-up boots, and studded leather jacket with patches from all the bands he loved were gone, but he held his head high again.

HEAR MY TRAIN
A COMIN'

Agustín gazed at the sky as he lay on the windshield of the dilapidated taco truck his father had abandoned. His legs were kicked up against the pointed iron gate that fenced off his uncle's duplex from their blighted neighborhood. Headphones clasped over his ears, he listened to the scorching bluesy numbers on the Jimi Hendrix Experience's *BBC Sessions*. It was a brisk Saturday afternoon. His mother was already drinking. The long summer was at hand. His last one before high school began, where bigger kids and more bullies awaited.

Once his stomach grumbled, Agustín jumped off the truck. He was short and chubby with full cheeks. The Latino boys at junior high called him "chanchito" and often coupled that with oinking sounds. He marched up the stairs to their flat, where he found his waifish mother sitting at the dining table while her latest boyfriend, Raúl, whistled in the bathroom. Her long, scraggly hair was dyed an unnatural-looking copper brown. She had green, catlike eyes traced with a thin eyeliner. Although she was in her late thirties, her pockmarked face was ragged as though she were approaching fifty. She drank from a large half-empty glass of rum and coke.

"I'm getting hungry," Agustín said.

"Go down to your aunt's for dinner," she said.

He walked to his bedroom. The TV blared a music video from Bandamax, her favorite channel. He hated how loud she played music from the television. One night, years before, Agustín stood in the hallway in his pajamas and said, "Do you *have* to play your music so loud?" She threw the remote control and it whizzed past his head, clanging off the wall. "You can set the volume however you want when you work and buy your own fucking TV," she said.

Agustín grabbed his library book, the latest *Jimmy Coates* action-packed adventure. He stepped out into the hallway just as Raúl emerged from the bathroom. He was a dark-skinned man in his late-thirties with stylish curly hair and bushy sideburns. He was a bartender at a cantina close to his Uncle Rudy's restaurant, where his mother waited tables. Like most of the boyfriends she had after his good-for-nothing father left them three years before, Raúl and his mother shared an affinity for alcohol.

"How's it goin', little man?" Raúl said, a cigarette tucked behind his ear.

Unsure of what to say to him, Agustín simply nodded. They stepped over to the living room.

"Mom, where's Isabel?" Agustín asked.

"Her friend's house."

"Okay, I'm going downstairs for dinner."

"Make sure you save us some!" Raúl said. "Your aunt cooks real good."

Agustín rolled his eyes once his face was turned away. He sped down the stairs and knocked on the door. By then he had one overarching goal in life: to get out of West Oakland and never return. He was tired of living in a neighborhood that was like a virtual version of *Minesweeper*, teeming with liquor stores and seedy street corners and parks that were best avoided. He was tired of living in a neighborhood where he didn't feel safe outside because he was afraid of getting mugged by other kids. He was tired of living in a neighborhood that never felt like home. And he was tired of living with his mother. For Agustín, West Oakland would always be a place where he and his family were banished once she alone could not afford the mortgage payments for their old house in San Pablo.

Aunt Gladys, his mother's older sister, opened the door. She wore a flowery apron. Her dark-brown hair was tied back in a bun.

"Hi auntie," Agustín said. "Can I come over?"

"Pues claro, pasale mijo," Aunt Gladys said, holding the door open. Agustín gave her a hug and a peck on the cheek.

Their living room walls were painted a bright-blue shade while the white ceiling in his mother's flat was peeling. Colorful textile rugs and framed panoramic posters of Mexico decorated Aunt Gladys's walls. His uncle's record collection of classic rock and Spanish crooners took up an entire shelf by their entertainment system. Crayons and coloring books were strewn all over their dining table. Pictures of his seven-year-old cousin, Manuelito, and their family from Oaxaca hung in the hallway.

"¿Quieres algo de tomar? There's water, Sprite, and some lemonade I just made."

Agustín took a seat at the end of their table. "I'll have some lemonade, please."

His aunt brought him a glass. He thanked her. Agustín watched her as she rinsed her hands at the sink, then she gently dried them before reaching into a large plastic bowl.

"What are you making?" he asked.

"Tamales. ¿Quieres ver?"

She lifted the lid from the pot on the counter. Agustín got on his tippy-toes to peer inside. It was filled with cornhusks soaked in water.

"You have to keep the husks wet otherwise they'll dry up and can't bend. Your mother's never made them before?"

"Nope. She makes enchiladas like you do, though."

"We learned that from your abuelita. We ate them all the time."

Back at the table Agustín flipped through his cousin's *Teenage Mutant Ninja Turtles* coloring book before opening his book. His mother never encouraged Agustín or Isabel to read, though it was a welcome surprise that he was such a bright student. Near the end of the school year, his US history teacher, Mrs. Lewis, had told him that she hoped he would continue to excel so he could get into a good school someday. This took him aback. Until that moment he had never considered college as a possibility. There was no precedent for it within his family. His mother and father did not graduate high school in Oaxaca. His mother and Aunt Gladys barely finished elementary school, since his grandparents pulled them out of school to earn money for their family. But once Mrs. Lewis explained that he could earn scholarships, or take out loans to pay for school, Agustín vaguely figured it could be his way out.

Aunt Gladys took a cornhusk from the pot. Like a delicate flower, she held it open in her palm then scooped a spoonful of masa and spread it over the cornhusk. Agustín watched her stuff it with vegetables and bits of chicken. There was a grace, a gentleness, to how she prepared them.

Why couldn't I have had Aunt Gladys for my mom? Agustín thought.

After they played a few hours of Nintendo with their cousin, Agustín and his sister, Isabel, stepped out of their aunt's flat to go back upstairs. Night was setting. Salsa music and raucous laughter blared from within. Although the front door was ajar, the screen door was locked. Isabel rapped on the house. Their mother staggered to the door.

"How you kids doin'?" she asked as they stepped in. Her breath reeked of rum. "Did your auntie make you dinner?"

"Yup, it was good," Isabel said dismissively. Her long, brown hair flowing behind her, she strode to her bedroom without acknowledging Raúl, who stood in the kitchen mixing a drink. Agustín hesitated, then he followed Isabel.

"Oye ven aqui," their mother shouted. "You didn't say hi to Raúl."

Isabel stopped. She slumped her shoulders and huffed.

"Hi, Raúl," she said in a monotone voice, leaning around the corner to wave to him.

Agustín nodded at Raúl. The siblings walked back to their rooms. He could feel his mother glaring at them. "Pendejos," he heard her say before he shut his bedroom door.

The next morning, Agustín creaked his door open. He peered over at his mother's bedroom. The door was closed. He waited to hear for any telltale snoring. There was none; Raúl had not spent the night. He figured she was probably hungover. Without Raúl around she was more likely to yell at them if they made any noise to disturb her.

He tiptoed down the hall to the bathroom next to his mother's bedroom. He sat on the toilet to urinate quietly then shuffled down the hall. The kitchen smelled like smoke. Cigarette ashes were scattered on the linoleum floor around the trash can. Empty bottles of Victoria and bottle caps littered the dining table. An empty drinking glass, an uneaten taco, and half of a burrito rested at his mother's usual spot. A small pile of coins and bills lay beside a paper bag stained with grease spots. Agustín counted it: four dollars and sixty-five cents. It must have been change Raúl or his mother left from the night before.

Since he couldn't turn on the TV for fear of waking her, Agustín went back to his room with a milk carton and a peanut butter and jelly sandwich in hand. He sat at his desk and turned his computer on. He glanced at his bookshelf, at the few books he owned. He had finished the *Jimmy Coates* book the night before. *If only I could get to the library I could get some more books*, he thought. That's when he got an idea: What if he walked to the

BART station and took a train to the Berkeley Public Library? Deirdre, his math tutor at the community center, told him the library was beautiful—that he *must* visit it. She said it was much larger than the West Oakland branch. With the money from the kitchen coupled with a few dollars he had, Agustín figured he had enough to buy a ticket to take him there and back. He had never taken public transportation by himself—and he had only been on BART once for a field trip. Unless something bad happened, his mother would never find out. Nor would his aunt or uncle. The worst that could happen is that a gang of neighborhood kids would roll up to him on their bikes and tell him to hand over his money.

Soon after, Agustín heard two knocks on his wall. It was Isabel's way of asking if he was awake. He knocked back thrice to signal that he was coming over. But just then he heard his mother's door creak open. He froze. He could hear her turn the shower on. *She's getting ready for work*, he thought. It was his chance.

He marched out of his bedroom, pocketed the money from the table, and retreated to his room. His heart thumped in his chest. He had never taken money from his mother. As he waited for her to walk out to the kitchen to see if she noticed the missing money, he looked up directions to the station. He jotted them down on the back of his hand. It wasn't far, but he didn't want to get lost on the way there, because he didn't want to look like he was lost. Not in his neighborhood.

Before long Agustín heard the shower turn off. He tucked the money into one of his sneakers. He took a breath and waited. A few minutes later his mother lumbered down the hall to the kitchen and knocked on his door before she swung it open. She stood in the doorway, wearing a bathrobe. Her long, wet, stringy hair fell down her back. Her eyes were bloodshot.

"I've got an afternoon shift today," she said. "Your aunt can make you food if you're feeling hungry. I'll bring home some leftovers."

"Okay, Mom," he said as she shut the door. Relieved, he sank back in his chair.

He dressed himself for his urban adventure: baggy shorts, a T-shirt, and his worn sneakers. He placed his library card in his pocket. Twenty minutes later his mother was out the door. Agustín and Isabel emerged in the hallway.

"Where are you going?" she asked, noticing his shoes.

"I'm going out. I'm walking over to the BART station. I'm going to try to take a train."

"*Why?* Where do you want to go?"

"I want to go to a library. A good one. I'm tired of being stuck here."

Isabel grimaced. Once they moved to West Oakland, Agustín never made friends like she did.

"Why don't you just wait for Mom to take you some other day?"

He shook his head. "I have to do this on my own."

"You better be careful."

"I will," he said, trying to believe his own words. "I wrote down directions."

Agustín flipped his hand and showed her the names of the streets he would have to traverse to reach the station. She smirked. "You're such a dork," she said.

Isabel stood in the hallway and watched him step out. He waved before closing the door. As he descended the steps, Agustín looked out to the street. There was no one in sight.

On his way out the front gate, he glanced at the pastoral landscape his father had painted on the side of his taco truck. Using a marker, Agustín had drawn black eyes and a gap tooth on the valiant ranchero riding a horse that was supposed to be his father. No one seemed to have noticed it, because no one ever brought it up. He opened the gate and stepped out.

Agustín marched along a chain link fence that closed off a large concrete lot that housed rows of enormous, graffiti-tagged pipes. He stared ahead with a cold, hard look—the facial expression he had learned in order to walk around his neighborhood. He stepped around an old mattress that had been lying on the sidewalk for weeks. Up ahead a car turned the corner, heading in his direction. He continued down the street as if he knew where he was going. Once the car passed, Agustín looked at the directions jotted on his hand. All he had to do was walk two blocks to the end of the street, round the corner, and continue onto 7th Street.

Once he reached the end of the block, Agustín crossed the street. Shards of brown glass lay by the curb. He stared at an abandoned Victorian with boarded windows and a front door with a "No Trespassing" sign. This was the farthest he had ventured on their street. He continued on, past a small Baptist church. As he rounded the corner, he heard a train in the distance. He saw its elevated tracks above the neighborhood. He looked back. He couldn't see their home.

Agustín heard some kids shouting inside a house. He bolted down the block, looking back behind him, but no one ran after him. He turned toward 7th Street. The train tracks loomed above, blocking the sunlight. The station was five long blocks away, but he was on a street with vehicular traffic, which made him feel safer.

He continued on past closed storefronts before he reached a liquor store. A rap song blared from the parking lot. Two men wearing sunglasses sat on the trunk of a black BMW. Agustín could not tell if they were watching him. He wiped his damp hands on his shorts. He continued on, making sure not to look at them. He listened to hear if they would follow him, but all he could hear was their music blaring. Soon after, he passed the parking lot, out of their sight, then he strode past a fenced-off field littered with discarded wrappers and empty bottles. Across the street an elderly black couple sat at a bus stop with their grocery bags. Once he saw the station's parking lot, Agustín grinned.

At the station he saw an agent sitting behind an encased booth with a newspaper spread before him. A young Caucasian couple pressed buttons on machines that read "BART tickets." He stepped over to a vacant one. Out of the corners of his eyes, he watched the young man put a bill into a slot then press some buttons until the machine spat out a ticket. Agustín watched them leave. He saw them pass through the tollgate after they slipped their ticket into a slot. He turned back to the ticket machine. He studied the screen then knelt to pull the money out of his shoes. The bills were damp. His hands were clammy. He unfolded a bill and slipped it into the machine's slot like he had seen the young man do. He jolted when it sucked up his dollar but sighed with relief when the screen told him he had a dollar credit.

In short time Agustín held a ticket with a five-dollar value. He stepped to the tollgate with ticket in hand. He held it to the side with the arrow pointing toward the slot. Like out of the sci-fi movies he loved, the gate doors parted when he slipped the ticket in. Once it popped out on the other end, he grabbed the ticket and darted across before the doors could snap shut.

Agustín came to a stop in the lobby. He stared at the escalators on both sides of the station. He had no idea where to catch a train to Berkeley. He stepped over to the station agent's booth. He stood there for a while before he knocked on the glass. The station agent slid over to peer down at him.

"Where do I catch the Berkeley train?" Agustín asked.

"Go up that escalator," the agent said, pointing at one.

Once on the train platform, Agustín glanced around at his unfamiliar surroundings. To his right, off in the distance, he saw Oakland's downtown skyline. To his left he saw the tallest apartment buildings in his neighborhood. He stared across at the other platform, which had more people waiting on the benches. He was afraid he was on the wrong side.

Down the platform Agustín saw a tall, slender man with wire-rimmed glasses. He wore a dark shirt that said "Danger: Educated Black Man." Agustín studied his face. He looked like a nice guy.

"Excuse me, sir," Agustín said to him. "Is this where trains to Berkeley come?"

"Yeah," he said. "You can take the next train and transfer onto one to Berkeley." The young man hesitated before asking, "Your first time on BART?"

Agustín peered past him. There were other people

around, including a young Caucasian woman sitting on a nearby bench with her bicycle.

"I'm going to visit my sister," Agustín said. "She goes to school in Berkeley. She's waiting for me at the station."

"That's cool."

He told Agustín there were no direct trains to Berkeley. He would have to transfer from a Pittsburg / Bay Point train to another one at a downtown station, but he'd show him where to catch it. Agustín nodded as if he understood everything the young man had explained.

Before long a train approached. Agustín took a step back as he watched car after car rumble by.

"See how it says Pittsburg / Bay Point?" the man said, nodding at an electronic sign that hung over the platform. "This is the train you want. My name's Lamar, by the way."

Agustín followed Lamar aboard. He took a seat by the doors. Agustín noticed the system map posted behind him. Lamar took a step to the side.

"We're right here," Lamar said, pointing at West Oakland on the map. "We're on a train that would take us all the way here."

Agustín nodded as he watched Lamar point at Pittsburg / Bay Point. After he studied the map, he stared out the windows. Off in the distance he could see the cranes at the Port of Oakland, although he didn't know what they were. Outside the sun shone brightly. The sky was clear azure. With both hands Lamar hung onto an overhead pole.

"So your sister goes to Berkeley?" Lamar asked.

"Yeah."

"That's a pretty good school. I tried to get in, but I wasn't accepted."

"You go to school?" Agustín said.

"I go to Cal State East Bay. It's in Hayward."

Other than Deirdre, Lamar was the first college student he had ever met.

The train rocked and slowed. Agustín whipped his head left and right as it rumbled into a tunnel.

"Don't worry, we're almost there," Lamar said.

The conductor got on the intercom to announce their arrival at the 12th Street station. Holding on to a pole, Agustín stood up. Lamar held out his hand to stop him. "Next station," he said.

Agustín stared at the parade of people stepping on and off the train. When they rolled into the 19th Street station, he noticed its brick walls were painted blue instead of red like at the previous station. Lamar waved him over. Together they disembarked once the doors opened. Side by side, Agustín followed him as they walked toward a stairwell. A train with open doors waited on the other side of the platform.

"That's your train," Lamar said, pointing at it.

Agustín slowed to watch him bound up the stairs. He followed the stream of people crossing the platform to the Richmond train. Once inside he clutched a pole by the doors. He looked around to see if anyone was staring at him. With the exception of a young couple sitting on a bench, everyone sat alone, staring off into space or down at their phones.

The train emerged from the tunnel. Towering concrete pillars supporting a freeway passed by. Beneath them Agustín saw the inner city unfold—the Victorian houses, expansive billboards, lush trees, and fences tagged with graffiti. The train swayed as it sped down the tracks. Another train rolled up beside them. He could see the murky outlines of people riding within it. Agustín smiled. It seemed as if the trains were racing each other.

Once they reached the Berkeley station, Agustín followed the people leaving the train. Together they ascended a small stairwell, where a group of Asian students stood and chatted in a circle. Agustín clutched the ticket in his pocket. At the tollgate he slipped it into the slot and grabbed it again. He examined the ticket. In small, faint print it read, "$3.05." He was amazed that the ticket told him how much money remained. He couldn't help but smile as he imagined how far that ticket could take him.

After he tucked it away, Agustín looked around the station lobby. He saw what appeared to be a street map. He stood before it and searched for the library. His eyes widened when he saw that it was only two blocks away.

Past an escalator he saw a young man with blonde dreadlocks sitting on a wooden box, strumming an acoustic guitar. His playing echoed through the station. A top hat stuffed with dollar bills rested at his feet. The young man sung a folk number as Agustín walked past him.

Agustín stepped onto the long escalator that led out of the station. Holding on to the handrail, he stood behind a line of people. He stared up at the sunlight shining through the dome of glass above. He leaned to the side, eager to see what awaited.

Acknowledgments

My love and thanks to my friends and peers who read these stories with their crafty eyes: Tara Dorabji, Rita Chang-Eppig, Scott Russell Duncan, Lisa D. Gray, Blanca Torres, Justin Goldman, Christopher Marnach, Judy Johnson-Williams, Sommer Schafer, Amelia Loulli, John Haggerty, Adam Smyer, and Jeff Chon.

My gratitude to Dini Duran Karasik and the editorial staff at *Origins*, Laura Roberts at *Black Heart Magazine*, and Ginger Murchison at *The Cortland Review*. Thank you to Michele Shaul at *Label Me Latina/o*.

Thank you to Lysley Tenorio for making me a better storyteller.

Thank you to Richard Basset for being one of the first to believe in my writing. Rest in peace, homie.

Thank you to my dear friend Tagi Qolouvaki for being my first devoted reader.

And my love and gratitude to my good lady, Maria, for putting up with my crazy ass.